Other La Caille Nous Titles

The Eye of the Tornado
0-9718191-6-5; Aug. 2003

Backfield in Motion
0-9718191-3-0; Nov. 2002

The Canon of Loose Canons
0-9718191-2-2; Nov. 2002

When He Calls
0-9647635-9-1; July 2002

Father's Footsteps
0-9718191-1-4; July 2002

Bard From Par Taken
0-9718191-0-6; June 2002

Water in a Broken Glass
0-9647635-7-5; Sept. 2000

When You Look At Me
0-9647635-6-7; June 2000

Temples
0-9647635-5-9; Feb. 1999

The Masks of Flipside
0-9647635-4-0; May 1998

Party Ain't Over Yet!
0-9647635-3-2; March 1997

The A# Blu's
0-9647635-2-4; Sept. 1996

My Baby's Father
0-9647635-8-3; April 2001 (revd.)

LoneWolf's Cry
0-9647635-0-8; Feb. 1996

Pick-Up Lines

Pick-Up Lines

Michael T. Owens

La Caille Nous

Edited by Guichard Cadet

Cover Photo: Ian O. Irving
Female Model: Nichole Howard
Male Model: Walter Pederson

Cover Design: Keith Saunders for Marion Designs

Library of Congress Cataloging-in-Publication Data

Owens, Michael T., 1975-
  Pick-up lines / Michael T. Owens.
     p. cm.
  ISBN 0-9718191-5-7 (pbk. : alk. paper)
  1. African American men--Fiction. 2. Dating (Social customs)--Fiction. 3. Atlanta (Ga.)--Fiction. 4. Young men--Fiction.
I. Title.
  PS3615.W47P53 2003
  813'.6--dc21

                          2003051489

La Caille Nous Publishing Company
PO Box 1004
Riverdale, MD 20738
www.lcnpub.com

Media & Distribution
328 Flatbush Avenue, Suite 240
Brooklyn, NY 11238
212-726-1293
media@lcnpub.com

In memory of my Auntie, Sylvia Jean Williams

ACKNOWLEDGMENTS

My journey from turning an idea into a full-fledged novel has been full of ups, downs, thrills, and more! But I definitely couldn't have done it without all of the support I received. With that in mind, I have tons of people to thank: God for giving me a talent and an opportunity to share it with others. My family for all of their support. Thank you, thank you, thank you, to my editor Guichard Cadet for believing in my work from day one and helping me shape this book into more than I initially envisioned. You're a cool brother with a great passion for what you do! Did I say thanks yet? Toey Farrie, you don't understand how much you helped me by offering your insightful input and constant encouragement. If you hadn't given me a kick in the pants, I probably would've never written this book! Kalyca A. Thomas, for your enthusiasm and willingness to help without hesitation. I wish I was as organized as you!

To my author friends: Karen E. Quinones Miller thanks for all of the knowledge you dropped on me. Thanks for answering every last one of my questions too—even if it meant listening until the wee hours of the morning! Zane, thanks for lending a helping hand. I really appreciate it. Michael Baisden, thanks for the words of advice. Daaimah Poole, thanks for your support. Sally Ramirez, the editing goddess, thanks for helping me tame the early rough draft of this monster. My Florida State University and FAMU peeps: Edwin & Katrina Hudson, Tyrone & Shawn Storr, Jonise & Jewell Crute, Rovall & Tonisha Washington, Albert Fiol, Marcus Evans, Natalie Barrett, Natasha Patterson, John Etienne, Travis Kennedy, Takiyah Salahuddin, Gil Black, Craig Cisek, Kristina Storr, and Steve Roberts. Vincent Hockett, for making my time in Atlanta all that and a bag of cool ranch Doritos! Thanks to the following for their helpful input, suggestions, and feedback: Kashon Forman, Kim Deschamps, Jessica Davis, Anna A. Horn, April Ellington, Nakita Carter, Lakiesha Carr, and Kenya Newman. Thanks to all of the crew at AALBC.com. Thanks to anyone else I may have missed, I still got love for you!

Michael T. Owens

1

Women outnumber men in Atlanta ten to one—and believe me, I've had my share. But what can I say? Ladies love me! I know what they wanna hear, when they wanna hear it, and how they wanna hear it. See, the secret is having a smooth opening line. I gotta million of them. Sometimes they work, sometimes they don't—success depends on the delivery. If the delivery is good, it can knock a chick off her feet. If the delivery is lame, then her fist will knock a man off his!

I'll be the first to admit sometimes the routine gets kinda old. Half the time I find myself approaching women simply outta habit and not 'cause I'm actually seeking anything. It seems like for every decent chick I meet, I gotta run through twenty lame ones. That's a shame. Shoot, I know how to treat a woman but I ain't trying to be no chick's second father. And I really ain't trying to be the 'Bank of Leron King' to these broads either. It would be nice if I could take the good qualities from each one and create a whole new bombshell chick. But then again, if I had magical powers like that, I'd put it in a can, sell it, and become a millionaire. In the meantime, I'm just Leron King, a twenty-four year old Security System Technician and wannabe novelist in Atlanta.

I'm not a big baller or anything but I do okay. My apartment doesn't have much furniture: a brown sofa, chair, coffee table, stereo, and a Playstation on the floor near the TV. The place ain't spotless but it ain't filthy either. Let's just say it's easy to tell a man lives here. Gotta nice-sized bedroom, a big bed, black sheets, and a stuffed puppy sitting between the pillows—chicks think it's cute. On the sides of the bed are tall wicker baskets with long colorful feathers sticking outta them. Sitting on top of the bookshelf, overlooking the room is an antique bust of Shakespeare. My English teacher gave it to me back in high school. Above my desk is a picture of Michael Jordan dunking. I wish I was out playing ball right now but I need to finish this chapter. Maybe some Viagra mixed with a lil' ginkoba will help me think harder— I've been typing the same page for an hour and a half. I finally decided to stop being lazy and actually sit down to write a book. Everybody always said I should. They said I write really good—really well, whatever. I've been trying to get a lil' writing done before heading out to kick it with the fellas tonight. If these chicks stop calling every ten minutes, maybe I can get something done.

"Hello?"

"Hey sexy, what are you doing?" I smack a hand against my forehead when I realize it's Tierra on the line—annoying, talk-way-too-much Tierra. I shoulda looked at the caller ID before picking up. She's a vegetarian chick studying massage therapy; we met at a self-improvement seminar. Now she calls, calls, and calls. If I tell her I'm sleepy—she'll still keep talking. If I tell her I'm tired—she'll still wanna talk. If I tell her I gotta piss—she'll stay on the phone and wait! I never heard anybody talk as much as this girl. I mean, I like a stimulating conversation, but this chick talks about nothing—nothing at all.

"Nothing much," I yawn, trying to give her a hint. "I just got in and I'm kinda tired."

"Oh, you poor thing. You want me to come and give you a free session?"

I made the mistake of letting her spend the night once. She's been trying to come back over ever since and I'm running outta excuses.

"I'm fine, I'm just gonna take a nap." It's a weak reply but it's the first thing to pop in my head.

"Well, I've gotten much better since the last time. I'm doing really well in my classes. We've been learning how to open, release, and channel the body's stored energy..."

"Oh, really?" Even though I'm not interested, I feel obligated to act like I am.

"...Yeah, but before energy can be released, the coccygeal, dorsal, lumbar, and cervical regions of the vertebral axis must be relaxed."

No, your mouth needs to be relaxed, I think to myself as she carries on.

"The secret is all in the fingers. You have to know how to use your fingers to promote the proper movement of energy. You should take a class too, you'd learn a lot—oh, did you just call me? I heard the phone ring five minutes ago, but I was painting my nails and I couldn't answer it in time."

Why did she call me and ask if I called her? I hate these stupid games. "No, it wasn't me."

"Oh," she responds, like she's surprised I didn't call. "Well, what are you doing tonight? Want some company?"

Even if I were stuck home alone watching the *All in the Family Marathon,* I still won't let her come over! "Me and my boys kickin' it tonight—probably hit a club or something."

"I think it's nice that you hang out with your friends sometimes. I don't have any problem with that. I'm not one of those women that need to be up under her man twenty four-seven. I believe in giving a man his space. I know I need my space too, so my girlfriends and I go shopping or out to dinner, things like that—just us women having fun." I'm short of breath just listening to her ramble. "Well, call me later on if you want, my girls are out of town and I'll be home all alone—all night."

I know why she's gonna be home all night. No man wants to listen to her mouth flapping nonstop! I already made that mistake once.

As she talks my ear off, I think back to the first time I went to her crib. She said she prepared a meal fit for a "King." When she answered the door, she looked so good; I wondered if she was dessert! Petite and fit, with the sun tattooed on her back, she had the clearest, most gorgeous skin I've ever seen.

"Hi, come in," she said cheerfully. I entered what looked like a museum. Incense burned low, releasing soothing fragrances, nude art covered the walls, and she didn't even have a television—she was one of those 'culturally aware' alternative chicks.

"I'm on a long distance call, I'll be done shortly. There's some finger food on the table, help yourself," she said, walking to her room.

A tray covered with sliced carrots, celery sticks, and whole-wheat crackers sat on the coffee table. I guess she thought I was a hamster or something. Passing on the *treats*, I casually walked around the living room. A huge oak bookcase sat in the corner loaded with thick books. *Wholistic Health Today, The Art of Reiki, Lifestyle Management,* and *Basic Reflexology Techniques* were some of the titles. I pulled outta book entitled *Metabolic Detoxification.* Tierra walked in as I read the back cover.

"Okay, I'm back—oh, *Metabolic Detoxification,* that's a good one," she said, standing with her hands on her hips. I nodded hoping to avoid a long explanation—a bad habit of hers. It didn't work. "... It tells you how to rid yourself of unwanted toxins so your body can function better..."

"Cool, sounds interesting." I quickly placed the book back on the shelf.

"...Detoxifying your body gives you renewed energy and vitality..."

Again, I nodded.

"...See, the body's toxins are stored mostly in the fat cells. As the individual cells shrink, the toxins are released and—"

"Mmm. Mmm. Something sure smells good, what's for dinner, sweet thing?" I asked abruptly to shut her up.

"My world famous barbecue."

I rubbed my hands together. "That sounds good."

"It is. You wash up, and I'll go in the pharmacy and get everything ready." She once told me why she called the kitchen a pharmacy but I wasn't listening. I guess it was a health freak thing. After washing my hands, I went in the kitchen to help speed things up—I was starving.

"You need any help with anything?"

"Um...just put the glasses on the table. Did you want to fix your own plate or do you want me to fix it?"

"You can fix it, it's no big deal."

"Okay. I only asked because some people don't like others fixing their food, that's all. I had a friend who used t—"

"I'm not too picky, I eat everything."

"Good."

After fixing my plate, she handed it to me and sat down with hers. Ready to dig in, I hesitated. Something looked strange. *What in the world is this?* I thought. *Did she just run in a forest and scoop up the first thing she saw?* Starving and impatient, I picked up my fork—I didn't wanna be an ungrateful guest. I smelled barbecue but didn't see any chicken or ribs for that matter.

"Okay, this may sound like a silly question, but where's the barbecue?" I asked, calm and relaxed.

"Leron, it's on your plate," she laughed.

Puzzled, the only recognizable thing on my plate was the rice. "Where?"

She leaned over and pointed it out. "Right there. That's barbecue tofu."

I tried to keep from showing disgust, but couldn't. "Barbecue tofu?"

"Yeah, try it. It's good, you'll like it. Besides, you'll eat anything," she said and smiled, resting a hand under her chin.

I eyed the food like it was a bad science experiment. "Hmm, and what's this?" I pointed to a leafy green spinach type dish.

"That's steamed kale...and that's curried cauliflower served over brown rice...and those are roasted chick peas with garlic and pine seeds. And I blended some fresh carrot and beet juice for us to drink."

Gritting my teeth, I realized I'd been hoodwinked. Suckered. Bamboozled. Shanghaied. Led astray. I'm a meat man and she was trying to feed me bark, twigs, and leaves? My facial expressions said it all.

She took a small nibble of her tofu. "Oh, come on it's not that bad, Leron. What kind of food do you normally eat?"

"Frozen dinners and red punch," I said proudly. Her nostrils flared and I felt another wordy lecture coming.

"Ewww, that's terrible! Those things are loaded with salt and saturated fats," she yapped. "...And red punch? That stuff isn't even made with real juice..." And yapped. "...It's full of sugar. You're just feeding the yeast in your system; and the more you feed it, the more it grows..." And yapped some more. "...You know yeast leads to prostate cancer and other health problems, right? My Uncle Ricky..." Blah. Blah. Blah. I tuned her out and ate my meatless meal—pissed!

I won't even bother mentioning what happened the rest of the night. Let's just say I left with sore ears and an upset stomach. I ended up home on the toilet late at night reading an old *Ebony Magazine*.

Slowly, I fade back into the telephone conversation.

"As fine as you are, you gonna be home alone on a Saturday night?" I ask, trying to sound a lil' interested, gotta keep all my options open. I don't believe in burning bridges—plus she has a bangin' body. She's a sweet girl but when she opens her mouth—that's a problem!

"Yes," she sighs, "you'd be surprised at how many girls like me spend Saturday nights at home...well, I don't want to hold you up; I know you're tired." As she talks, I think *when did my being tired ever matter?* "I'm going to let you get some rest; you're going to need it if we hook up later tonight! Be good."

I hang up, write some more, and then pick out my clothes for tonight. Gotta be sharp, I only got one number last time so I gotta redeem myself.

▼

Around 10:00 p.m., me and the guys stop at a burger joint before hitting the club scene. The place smells like French fries and old cooking oil but we're so hungry, it won't spoil our appetites. The chicks behind the counter are cracking jokes and cursing at each other while a short Puerto Rican dude works the drive-thru window. Me and my boy Spurt are standing at the counter waiting to place our orders. Spurt looks like a six-foot two stick figure, scratching his thick cornrow braids, trying to figure out what to get. I know he's not even going to wash his hands. He's been my boy since the third grade and outta all the years I've known him, I ain't never seen him wash his hands. He's cool peeps, just don't shake his hand or eat after him. Follow those two rules and you'll be fine. James is his real name but we call him Spurt 'cause he used to be the short kid back in ninth grade. During the summer of our sophomore year, he had a crazy growth spurt, shot up like four inches. So, everybody started calling him "Spurt."

"I'm starving!" he says, smacking his lips.

"Can I take your order?" asks the cashier, adjusting her one-inch ponytail.

Spurt smiles and says, "Girl you can take my order, my house, *and* my car with yo sweet self. What's yo name, Sugar?"

She points to the crooked nametag on her shirt. "It sho' ain't no sugar!"

I dunno why Spurt does this. He sees the girl is pissed off; she doesn't even wanna be at work, let alone be bothered; and he comes in talking all loud and country, trying to holler. He can't get a clue if it came in a can. I guess rejection turns him on.

He looks at her nametag and scratches his chin. "Tuh-mare-rah?"

"Tamara!" she snaps back, rolling her eyes.

"Oh, *Tamara*, my bad. Tamara, if you was a hamburger, they would call you the McBeautiful! You gotta man, Tamara?"

"Yes! Now can I please take your order?"

"You ain't' got no man, you just saying that!"

"Just tell her what you getting, Spurt!"

"Lee, she ain't got no man. I'm tellin' you she just saying that. She just don't wanna holler 'cause her boss lady standin' right there."

I should be used to this by now. Sometimes he acts like he was dropped on the head four times as a baby, but he still gets women. I dunno how. Last year before he started working at the car shop he didn't have a job. I went down to the unemployment office with him, sat back and watched him get two phone numbers. Two! What woman in her right mind meets a guy in the unemployment office and gives him the digits? I dunno how he pulled that off, but he did. And believe me, he bragged about it for two weeks. I guess some chicks dig the loud, clueless, aggressive type.

Finally, we get our food and join Dave, Ra'ed, and X who are already seated and eating.

Dave's shaggy hair is brown this week. Last week it was blonde...I think. He's wearing the same red double knit shirt he wears every other weekend and it's soaked in cologne. With outta doubt, he's the whitest of all the whitest white boys I know. He has no rhythm, he's always happy, and is never broke! He doesn't work, though. He lives off money from a trust fund his granddad left him when he died. He kinda just does whatever. He was trying to be a rapper last month and a sculptor the month before that. Sitting in his garage is $4000 worth of art equipment and supplies, collecting dust. Now he's on some self-exploration tip and he's leaving for a mission in Ethiopia soon. I'm just surprised Ra'ed didn't sign up to go too. Him and Dave are always hanging together even though their backgrounds are as different as mayonnaise and mustard.

Ra'ed is Indian from India someplace but he has more soul than some brothers I know. I'm cool with his folks too. I've eaten there a couple of times—Mrs. Naseem can cook! Half the time I never know what I'm eating, but it tastes good. Now that I think about it, I don't even wanna know! He's an aspiring actor who kinda reminds me of an Indian Elvis 'cause he always wears button up shirts and keeps his hair slicked back. He must use a whole bottle of gel every time we go out. Maybe he'll stick with the acting thing. He's pretty hyped about it, so I'm supporting him. I support all his wild ideas; like when he became a paramedic then quit 'cause he had a weak stomach. And I can't forget the time he sold health care products—I bought a case of oat bran fiber pills to help him meet quota. Right now, my cabinets are still full of that mess. If anyone needs a good colon cleansing—I got the hook up! But I guess that ain't really nothing to brag about.

Then you got my man Xavier Spivey III. Man, we just call him X for short. You'll accidentally bite your tongue trying to say his whole name. Xavier Deshayon John Spivey III. I can't believe somebody named their kid 'Xavier.' I mean, maybe the first time—okay, but two more times after that? That's crazy! He's a trip, though. Smart too. In high school, teachers didn't like him much 'cause he always disrupted class—but could still answer any question. We talking brains, man. But he got more enjoyment from acting a fool from than acing tests. But unlike me, he did enough work to make it to college. Now he's some Computer Software Technician or something. I dunno, but he banks. Gotta smooth ride, rims and all that, but he's still the same dude—a straight clown with a ghetto fabulous name. But I can't talk. My name doesn't scream power and respect either—but I gets mine, don't worry.

We're debating on where to kick it tonight. But every time we plan something, we either don't do it or it doesn't work out how we planned. I already know how the night is gonna go: we're gonna go to a club and holler at the honies to see who gets the most numbers. It ain't even close. And besides, only three of us are "competing." Dave is too scared to talk to the ladies unless he's sloppy drunk. And X has a girl already. He always fronts like it ain't all that, but he's probably gonna marry her.

Me, Spurt, and X wanna roll out to The Garden 'cause it's always packed on Saturday nights, the honies are off the meter, and the drinks are cheap. But Dave and Ra'ed keep talking about going to this jive strip club on Cheshire Bridge Road called the Gentlemen's Lair. They might as well rename that joint Ra'ed and Dave's Lair 'cause they're in there all the time paying for something they can see for free. They must've been breastfed babies 'cause they sure love them!

2

"It's on tonight!" Spurt hollers outta the passenger side window. We left the burger joint not too long ago and now we're exiting off I-75 onto 14th Street, headed downtown to The Garden. Traffic is bumper-to-bumper with flashy cars, sports utility vehicles, limos, motorcycles, and occasional station wagons with elderly couples accidentally caught in the congestion. It's a hot night, a lil' after eleven o'clock and it seems like everyone in Fulton County is out looking for a good time. Dashing out in front of cars, illegally crossing the street, yelling and screaming—people are everywhere. The hottest hip-hop, reggae, and house music pumps outta rides. Passing cars stop, squeal, and jerk as guys check out the honies. Horns are blowing; heads are hanging outta windows, gazing at chicks walking huddled together. We've circled the club three times already. If we pass that bum on the corner holding a sign reading: *Why lie? I need money for beer* or those same posters promoting some corny new rap artist, I might lose it—we all might—so we better find a parking spot soon.

"What about th—ah never mind, that ain't a spot," Spurt says.

"X, there's one over there," Dave says, pointing to a spot.

"Man, I can't fit my truck in there!"

I pull a twenty-dollar bill from my pocket. "Yo, let's just pay the ten dollars and park." They would rather circle the block fifty times looking for a space instead of paying ten sorry dollars for a spot. They also know that I'll eventually breakdown and pay for parking myself.

"Here, man."

"True, good looking out." X takes the money and circles back around to get a space.

Dave points at this tall redbone wearing skintight leather pants. "Ra. Ra, look at that! A beautiful black queen from the mother land."

Ra'ed nearly breaks his neck trying to see. "I wish I were your panties so I could hug sunshine!" he yells in her direction. She flicks him off and keeps walking. "Ouch, no love at all! You're not all that anyway."

Spurt leans outta the window to get a better view at these two thick girls. "Hey y'all, look at shorty with the hair."

I look over the front seat. "Which one?"

"Shorty with the hair, the one with the blue shirt."

"She's all right."

"All right? Man, please. Look at that cornbread booty!" Spurt holds his chest and fakes a heart attack. "Oh, lawd baby girl, what'cha doin' to me?" We pull beside them. He shouts outta the window, "I wanna have *yo* baby!" She laughs and walks faster. "That's me y'all! I'll see her in the club."

X pays the parking attendant and eases into a space.

"Hey, it's eleven forty-five. If we get in before twelve it's free," Ra reminds us. We're too busy being cool and relaxed to care.

"Dave, you remembered your ID this time?" I ask. He's notorious for forgetting his identification.

"Yeah, yeah I got it, relax."

We stand in line checking out the sites. The music becomes more distinct the closer we inch to the entrance, energy building up inside begins to trickle outside.

I tap my feet to the beat. "Fellas, I'm telling you now, I'm getting a phone number for every dollar I spend on admission!"

Spurt puts his hand on my shoulder. "We'll see, playboy."

After twenty minutes in line, we make it inside. Ra'ed is pissed 'cause we didn't make it inside before twelve. He's funny. He'll give half of his paycheck to strippers but complains about having to pay a cover charge at a nightclub.

The Garden used to be an old warehouse back in the day. Now, it's a restaurant during the day and one of the hottest spots in town at night. The orange glow-in-the dark walls trimmed in green vines and leaves give the building as much character as the people in it. The crowd is...well, diverse to say the least. Gathered around the dance floor are: ghetto women sporting two-tone weaves and halter tops; guys wearing their church clothes; rough-looking chicks smoking cigars; and thugs wearing wife-beaters and baggy jeans. In the corner, several gay dudes practice dance moves—two artsy chicks cheer them on; a big goofy dude hovers over his girl; and another gay guy entertains six fine chicks at the bar. It ain't too packed right now and people are moving freely. Some are dancing, others watching.

Me, Spurt, Ra, and Dave leave to get drinks while X stays behind, chillin' next to the speakers. He promised his girl he'd cut down on drinking.

We walk back over to X. Me and Dave have huge 'I got liquor' smiles on our faces, Ra'ed is lip-sync'ing to himself, and Spurt is stirring his drink, nodding to the music.

"Tonight is gonna be a good night," he says, checking out the groups of ladies walking in. Guys standing around the entrance wait to take their pick while the bouncers watch on the sides.

"Look," X laughs, pointing towards the door.

Like army ants raiding a Sunday picnic, these four, short, white tee-shirt wearing dudes march in like they own the place. We all burst out laughing.

"Look at these fools!"

"That's the five-four and under crew runnin' thangs," Spurt jokes.

X strokes his goatee. "More like Snow Black and the four dwarfs."

After an hour of hanging around, things heat up. The music thumps louder than ever. The crowd's electricity flows in hypnotic unison. Me and Spurt disappear in the crowd to look for some honies to brush up on. He points out two standing near the entrance. They smile as we approach.

Spurt leans over and says in my ear, "You take the skinny one, I got the thick one." He eyes the thick chick from head to toe then blurts out, "Hey shorty, you wearin' 'dem pants! Can I buy you a drink or do you just want me to give you the money?" I shake my head outta embarrassment as the girls walk away. "Oh, okay, it's like that? I was just tryin' to make you feel good—mmm, hey cowgirl!" he says to a chick walking by wearing a cowboy hat. "My name Spurt. You might wanna remember that 'cause you'll be screamin' it later on. Look here, baby, you probably don't think I'm the finest guy in here, but I'm the only one talking to *you*. Let's dance." He pulls her by the arm, leading her to the floor.

Ra'ed is sitting at a table talking to a girl, while Dave stands next to X against the back wall, steadily drinking. I think I can use another drink myself. I make a quick dash to the bar to reload. As I'm walking away, I notice a super fine chick by the deejay booth. I saw her earlier too and I've wanted to step to her all night but guys have been swarming her like ants on a sugar cube. After we make eye contact, I leave to try my luck.

I step to her and say a couple of lines. She responds in a strong Caribbean accent. "Oh, you're a smooth one me see," she sways to the rhythm, "cute too."

"Not as cute as you, Caribbean queen, can I be your king for a day?"

"Come." She snatches my arm and leads me to the dance floor. I don't mind her aggressiveness—less work for me. Smooth and sensual, she dances very close. One hand around my waist, the other behind my neck, she becomes my skin working me until sweat pours—especially during the deejay's reggae set. Both my hands are locked around her shapely Jamaican hips. We dance until the set ends. I get her number and head back to meet the fellas.

"It's off the hook tonight," I say, sipping another rum and coke. Normally I don't drink so much, but I worked hard this week, plus X is driving so it's all good.

"I gotta number already," Spurts says. "But she acted like she ain't want me to have it." He examines a number scribbled on a crumbled piece of paper, "It's probably fake."

"I haven't drunk enough yet. Check with me an hour from now," Dave says. His speech is starting to slur but he keeps on drinking.

"Oh lawd, that's the jam! I'll holler at y'all." Spurt heads to the center of the dance floor. I dunno why he rushed out there; he's not a good dancer at all. He has a stupid dance where he sticks his tongue out, nods his head up and down, and pumps his fist like he's blowing a train horn. It doesn't matter if the music is fast or slow; he always does the same dance. To make matters worse—he rarely stays on beat. But nobody can tell him he's not jammin.' I hit the dance floor too. I don't even like the song that much but my drink got me feeling kinda nice. I weave in and out, protecting my glass from the wild crowd when I see a dark-skinned chick groovin' alone.

"WHO ARE—" I stop and catch myself 'cause I'm talking way too loud. I must be a lil' more buzzed than I thought. I lower my voice and finish my sentence. "...Who are you hiding from?"

"No one," she moves her hips to the melody. "My girlfriend left me to go dance."

"...What's your name?" I ask.

"Anesia."

"I'm Leron, but you can call me...tonight." When she smiles, I step closer. "How about we get on the dance floor, maybe we'll bump into your girl."

"Well, I don't know if I—"

I take another sip from my glass. "I know you didn't spend your money to come here and dance in a corner by yourself! C'mon, girl!"

I grab her hand and wade towards the dance floor. After some high energy dancing and a lil' small talk, we exchange numbers and then I jet back to the fellas.

Dave stumbles up to me with bloodshot hazy eyes, clutching another brew. He holds up four fingers and yells, "Three, baby! Three numbers!" Pale and covered with red blotches, he swaggers side to side. "WHOO! They just can't tell me 'no' tonight! They can't!"

I know I'm kinda tipsy myself, but this dude is sloppy, sloppy drunk. I turn to Ra. "Calm that nut down."

"What do I look like, his mother?"

Dave yells again, "P-P-Par-taaay!" He accidentally bumps a woman walking past. "...Hey baby, how about you sit on my lap and we can talk about the first thing that pops up?"

She rolls her eyes, sucks her teeth, and keeps walking. "Leave me alone white boy. You don't have anything I want."

He yells as she walks away. "Do you have any white in you? If not, you want some?"

"Yo, Dave chill, man."

"How many numbers you got, Lee...Leeeron...?" Dave asks with watery eyes and bloated cheeks.

"Stand up!" Spurt grabs him by the shoulders standing him upright. All of a sudden, the fool pukes on the floor.

"What the—?"

"Man!"

"Oops, ha, ha," he wipes his mouth on his shirt, "Sorry guys..." He just spoiled the whole mood for the night. Spurt has a few choice words for him as we head for the exit. X clears the way while Dave staggers between me and Ra. Tonight is shot. My head is hurting anyway. I ain't drinking so much next week.

3

My new vanilla warmth fragrance floats through the cool air, making the whole bedroom smell sweet and edible. The television tuned to my usual Wednesday night shows, and radio playing classic R&B, sound like chaotic gibberish in the background but I'm not paying close attention to either. I have to get dressed. I keep running back and forth between the closet and the mirror in the vanity area trying to find the perfect dress. I stop in front of the mirror to look myself over. My light skin seems brighter than usual; my curled mid-shoulder-length hair looks fluffy and light. "You're gorgeous, Mrs. Michelle Colbert," I say out loud for the millionth time, adjusting my dress, making sure it hugs in the right places. "Mrs. Michelle Colbert," I sigh again. I like hearing how my first name sounds with Gregory's last. I didn't hesitate when he asked me to be his wife. There was a time when he'd walk barefooted through broken glass if I asked him to. Attractive, successful, and a good listener—he really has it together. Unfortunately, things have slowly gone downhill since the day I said, "Yes."

I never had to deal with anything like this in my life. For the most part, everything has always gone well. I finished high school in the top percentile, graduated college with honors, fell in love and got engaged. I always wanted to get married in my mid-twenties and everything seemed on schedule. But here I am, twenty-four years old and still finding myself—that's just ridiculous, depressing too. But I don't feel like thinking about that. Tonight I just want to relax and have fun.

I decided to wear my black spaghetti strap dress with the high cut split. Greg loves when I wear it with my diamond stud earrings. The only problem is I've searched all three bedrooms and still can't find them. I wish I knew where I put them because he is on his way and I want everything to be perfect. Lately his job has been *extremely* demanding. We haven't made love in over a month, and I can't remember the last time we went out. I want to be supportive but not at the expense of my own happiness.

When the doorbell rings, I anxiously rush to answer. Greg's golden wire frame glasses look very dignified against his smooth dark skin. When he walks inside, his alluring cologne follows closely. He is irresistible. I know I'm getting some loving tonight! He gives me a weak peck on the cheek and immediately goes to the bedroom and plugs up his laptop computer. An hour later, he is still typing away. Occasionally he will look up, scratch his forehead, and continue. I have to strain my ears to hear the television because of his heavy fingers pecking away. Finally, I give up, mute the volume, and imagine the dialogue.

I made him promise me tonight. That's why I asked him two

weeks ago to set aside some time for us. Once again, he let his job interfere. Once again, I'm lying in bed holding my pillow waiting for him to finish. All I wanted was dinner and a movie—nothing fancy. But right now, I'll settle for leftovers and *The Lifetime Channel*.

"Honey, how much do you have left?" I try my best not to sound agitated or upset—even though I am. It doesn't matter. He ignores my question. "Honey, are you almost done?"

"Huh? Yeah," he mumbles without missing a stroke.

I flip the channel to a couple gazing deeply into each other's eyes. The man softly traces the woman's hairline as if he's drawing an invisible halo. He whispers how breathing is meaningless without her. She feels the same. They kiss. Then he tells her how he would give up everything just to wake up beside her forever—at least that's what I imagine. I flip through every channel several times. I'm not watching television anymore; television is watching me. Throwing the remote to the edge of the bed, I get up and put on my *Greatest Slow Jams* CD. I try to do a little sexy dance but my joints crack and pop from lying around so long. Besides, Greg isn't fazed by me or Teddy Pendergrass' *Turn Off the Lights* playing in the background.

"Why don't you take a rest, baby?" I massage his shoulders to loosen him up.

"No. Not right now, I can't."

"You've been working too hard, honey. You don't want to relax?"

"Maybe later, I have to finish debugging this program." He scratches his head, "I keep getting these error messages and I can't figure out why."

I kiss the left side of his neck. "Well, why don't you rest and take a stab at it later?"

"No, now!"

"Come on honey. Come lay d—"

He slams the laptop closed and springs from the chair. His glazed eyes are focused dead on me. "I said I can't! What don't you understand, Michelle?"

"I'm just trying to help."

"I don't need help! I'm trying to get some work done—stop nagging me!"

I feel each of his hot words thrust in my face. That's it. I can't take this anymore. "WORK, work, work. It's always about work!" I say, shaking my head.

"What do you mean al—?"

"Always! That's all you care about. I have to go to work early, I have to work late; I can't come over because I have too much work to do. What about me, your fiancée? Do you care about me?"

"What kind of dumb question is th—?"

"Dumb? Dumb? Now, I'm dumb too?"

"That's not what I meant. Baby, you know I care about you. If I didn't, I wouldn't have asked you to be my wife." He places a hand on my shoulder.

"I can't tell! You touch that stupid laptop more than you touch me!"

"I—"

I cut him off before he can reply. "Greg, you promised. You promised we would finally spend some time."

"Baby, I know, I know. It's just that this project is huge. If I don't finish this program by the deadline, the company loses the contract!"

"What about losing me?"

He places his hands around my waist, pulling me closer to his wide chest. "Don't talk like that. I love you."

"If you love me then promise me you won't touch that laptop again tonight."

He rubs his head and sighs. "Baby, you know I have to finish debugging th—"

"...Promise me you won't touch that laptop again tonight!" I repeat slow and firm. He shifts his eyes to avoid direct eye contact. His jaw muscles tighten when he grits his teeth. Suffocating air magnifies the silence.

"Baby, I have to debug th—"

"GET OUT!"

"Michelle, I—"

"Get your computer and get out!" I charge after him to the front door.

He stops and turns around. "I'm doing this for us, can't you see that?" He sounds so pathetic. All I want to see are his taillights when he backs out of the driveway.

"Out!"

"Michelle, I love you. I love—" His voice muffles when the door slams in his face, he's still pleading. Trying to hold back the tears, I walk to the bedroom. My CD still plays, unmoved by what occurred. I don't mind because I need the company. I lie on the bed, snuggle tight with a pillow and my stuffed Panda bear. Fully-dressed, hair curled, perfume smelling sweet—I'm beautiful—but no one knows, and no one cares. A light heaviness swells in my chest. My eyes moisten as I stare at the blank television, struggling to keep my mind from wandering. I quickly lose the will, drifting back to the television show with the man and woman. The looks in their eyes, the magnetic sensuality in their touches was so passionate. I had that. *We* had that. Tears stroll down my face and I don't care to wipe. I take a deep breath and release. I'm anxious for tomorrow. Sometimes a new day makes the night before not seem as bad. I close my burning eyes and let Marvin Gaye sing me to sleep.

▼

The next day at lunchtime, almost everyone at the office is eating at their cubicle, working, or in the production department making last minute changes to client advertisements. I'm one of the few people who have an actual office and I've been in here working like a maniac. Thursday is the busiest day of the week for us, deadline day. The phone stays glued to my ear to make sure advertisements are placed in the Sunday newspapers on time.

"When can I expect to proof those display ads? I need them on my desk no later than three-thirty today." I balance the phone between my ear and shoulder while checking the media schedule, "I know I'm asking for a lot but—" Mrs. Harriet Feinstein, my Account Team's Assistant, knocks lightly and enters. She's an older Jewish woman, full of wisdom, with the spirit of a twenty-two year old. "...Just pull some strings or something, I'll follow up with you later, bye." Mrs. Feinstein has a concerned motherly stare. "Did the copier break again?" I ask. "I'm calling to get that thing serviced right away."

"No, no the copier is fine," she assures me as she sits down.

"Oh, well, what's up?"

"I dunno hon,' you tell me," she probes with precise, older woman inquisitiveness. We share a unique relationship. When I first moved to Atlanta she helped me adjust. Whether a mother figure, older sister or just one of the girls, she is always around when I need her. "You haven't been your normal animated self lately," she says, folding her arms. "What's wrong? Did you and Gregory have another fight, sweetie?"

I hesitate before answering. "Yes, Mrs. Feinstein, I don't know what to do. Things just aren't how they used to be. He's so absorbed by his work that I'm almost nonexistent. I don't even know if he's the right one for me anymore. And I don't want to marry the wrong person."

Her face glows with warm compassion. "I understand, sweetie. But it will pass. These kinds of things happen in relationships," she takes my hand, pressing it gently. "He's a good man, Chelle, and he loves you dearly." Her calm, raspy voice sounds certain. But I'm not.

"...Sometimes I'm not so sure. How did you know that Mr. Feinstein was truly in love with you?"

She stands and sticks out a leg. "Honey, with these legs, he didn't have a choice!" We laugh. I feel a little better. Mrs. Feinstein is the sassiest senior citizen in Atlanta—a title she would gladly accept—she's a real mess!

"You're so bad. Bad girl, Mrs. Feinstein!"

"You better believe it!"

Looking at my desk clock showing twelve-fifteen reminds me of my one o'clock client meeting. I thank Mrs. Feinstein for her advice and rush out of the office as fast as my high heels will take me. I would run but that isn't feminine. My handbag swings on my shoulder; my briefcase and coat are in one hand, my cell phone in the other. I swing around the corner and bump into a guy in a brown jumpsuit with a thick tool belt. He's about six-one with dark brown skin and broad lumberjack shoulders. His freshly cut low fade and thin sideburns are edged meticulously. He's not huge but I can tell he keeps fit. He definitely doesn't look like most maintenance guys I've seen.

"Sorry, that was really clumsy of me," I apologize, trying to gather my folders, weekly planner, and notepad scattered across the marble floor.

"Did it hurt?"

"Not really, I just banged my arm a little; I'm fine, thanks for asking."

"Not that! I mean, did it hurt when you fell from heaven?" He looks at me and smiles. I feel uneasy as his cinnamon brown eyes swallow me whole. He definitely caught me off-guard. I wasn't expecting a pick-up line—especially since I'm obviously pressed for time.

Trying to seem unaffected, I give him a half of a half smile. "Oh, uh, if that's a compliment, thanks."

"You're *very* welcome. My name's Leron, and you are?"

"Really in a rush—I've got to go, thanks for your help."

"Sure. Anytime...*anyplace*," he says under his breath. I know he is watching me hurry towards the double doors, but I don't care about looking pretty anymore—now I'm *really* late—I run out the lobby.

4

"Friday night...just got paid!" I sing on an imaginary microphone, dancing to the room. By now, the carpet is covered with wet footprints 'cause I just got outta the shower. The only reason I quit dancing is to do my Mr. Olympian poses in front of the mirror. I feel kinda good tonight. Hopefully, things will go better than they did last Saturday. Just to be safe, I'm driving my own ride so I won't have to leave early if Dave pukes again.

Spurt called before I left the house to tell me he ain't hanging tonight 'cause he's staying home with his son. Meka, his ex-girl, is trippin', talking about ever since they broke up he hasn't spent enough time with him. So, his son is spending the night, and tomorrow him and Spurt are going to Six Flags.

Around eleven o'clock, I meet up with X, Ra, and Dave at a fast food chicken spot. Dave is telling us more about the trip he's taking to Africa. I'd be interested some other time, but right now, I rather find out where we're clubbin.' I interrupt and ask everybody if they wanna try out this new spot on Courtland Avenue. I heard they had separate rooms for hip hop, R&B, and reggae.

Ra shakes his head. "Me and Dave are going to the Gentlemen's Lair, yo."

"Don't y'all get tired of that place? You can only look at titties for so long. And half the strippers there look like they fell out of an ugly tree and hit every last branch," X says.

I nod in agreement.

Dave hops in, "I can look at tits twenty-five hours a day, eight days a week. Tits here, tits there, tits everywhere, especially in Africa!"

I guess I should be glad Ra'ed and Dave the puke boy are going to the Gentlemen's Lair tonight—I don't have to worry about nobody messing up my night. I look at X. "You the only one left, man. What's up?"

He swallows the last bit of his chicken sandwich and says, "I'm game, but I have to stop by Lisa's first. I'll call you when I get ready to leave." Soon as he said *stop by Lisa's*, I knew he probably wasn't going anywhere. I know from experience that anytime a woman is involved in any way, things never go right—ever! Something about a soft voice, voluptuous curves, and a plump onion makes a brother lose all sense of time! In the words of Spurt, 'It's McBeautiful!'

"I think Lisa has you whipped," Dave says.

Ra'ed jumps in with his best imitation of Lisa. "Xavier do this... Xavier do that... Xavier don't eat that, it's bad for you...Xavier sit up straight, ha."

X isn't amused at all. Actually, I think he's a lil' upset. I can tell 'cause he has a lil' wrinkle in the center of his forehead. Whenever that happens, I know he's bothered.

"Shut up Muslim boy, before I force-feed you a pork sandwich."

We all start cracking up.

Ra is about dark as me but he turns red in the face. "You got me, yo. You got me."

After we finish eating, Dave and Ra bounce to the Gentlemen's Lair, X dips to Lisa's, and I go home.

▼

I've been chillin' on the couch wasting time, playing Playstation, waiting for X to call and let me know what's up. But I just realized I had my cell phone off all this time. He probably called already. I check my messages to see. He didn't call yet but some chick I met at the Garden did:

"Hi Leron, this is Anesia, we met at the Garden last Saturday. I just called to see if you wanted to catch a movie or something if you're not busy. I know it's short notice so if you can't, I understand. Either way, call me."

Hmmm. Anesia...Anesia, I think to myself. The name definitely sounds familiar; I just can't match a face to it. But if we exchanged phone numbers she has to be fine. I don't talk to any ugly girls! Maybe I'll check her out if nothing else is popping off, see if she's talking about anything.

12:27 a.m. I haven't heard from X yet! I would call him but I ain't trying to interrupt his groove. Bored and antsy, I hop on the computer to write a lil' and check my email. If I don't hear from him after that, I know it's a lost cause.

Every now and then, I chat with my peeps back home in Manchester, New Hampshire. I see two online right now. TooNice911 is my dawg, Joe; he's always online. But Nhprincess? That's my homegirl Femia Watts. She used to be my lil' girlfriend when I was a kid. She's always had a cute girlish face and when she smiles, you can't help noticing her two dimples—the left one doesn't show as much as the right. I have a couple of pictures she sent but I haven't seen her in person since I was eighteen. Even though she's cute, sweet, and smart, nothing ever became of us—timing was always bad. When she got accepted to the University of New Hampshire, we lost contact for a while. This past year we began communicating again.

LeronK: <Psssssst...hey little girl, want some candy?>

Nhprincess: <Roooooooooon!!!!!! What in the world are you doing online this late?>

LeronK: <Fefeeeeeeeeee! What up? I was just checking my email and I saw you online, so I said HEY!>

Nhprincess: <Well, HEY to you too! I'm surprised you're not out chasing women!>

LeronK: <Who me? LOL. You're right, I should be out but I'm waiting for my boy to call.>

Nhprincess: <Knowing you, it probably doesn't matter. I bet you have two or three girls lined up just in case!>

LeronK: <Ha. Ha. Whatever girl! How's your boyfriend?>

Nhprincess: <We broke up.>

LeronK: <WHAT? What happened?>

Nhprincess: <I have to go. I'll tell you later on. I don't feel like typing it.>

I thought Femia and that dude were gonna be together forever. The way she talks about him and all the things he does for her, I thought they'd never break up. I feel a lil' bad for her, though. She's really intelligent, caring, and easygoing, but she probably gonna end up with a scrub. Most of her boyfriends were some straight-up losers. They took her for granted but she would always make excuses for them. When she was in high school, she called me crying after the homecoming dance. Her boyfriend got mad and refused to take her home 'cause she wouldn't have sex with him. The next day at school, he was kissing some chick right in front of her. I couldn't wait until summertime so I could come up there and teach the cat a lesson. But Femia kept rationalizing, saying she knew sex was all he wanted. She said it was her fault and she shoulda never went with him. I didn't care about all that. He still shouldn't have treated her like that. By the time summer came, she had another boyfriend and all was forgotten. I still wanted to "talk" to the guy but she convinced me not to.

She dated more losers after him. Her first boyfriend in college was a shoplifter and tried to get her to lie when the cops busted him. She wouldn't. When he posted bail, he started stalking her and making threats. She had to get a restraining order. After that, she told me a lame excuse about him not having positive role models when he was growing up. That's why he acted like that. Whatever. I've wanted to confront all the scrubs she's dated. But who knows what might've happened, so I just stayed away. A person can always say what they will and won't do, but it's hard to tell until the moment actually comes.

But this new cat seemed cool. He treated her like royalty. He bought her flowers, jewelry—the whole nine. She was really in love with him. She says they broke up 'cause they aren't compatible. Honestly, they probably broke up 'cause she ain't used to being treated so well—I bet she didn't know how to react; and that probably caused a lot of stress in their relationship.

I shut down the computer to check my house phone voicemail. Two messages are waiting. One from Tierra—I'm glad she got my voicemail 'cause I ain't in the mood to hear her squeaky voice twangin' all in my ear; X left the other:

"Sup man, it's X. Sorry it took so long to get back at you. I can't make it tonight. Lisa wants to stay up and watch movies and I'm trying to stay on her good side, you know how it is. One."

Watching movies? I bet she's got him watching the *Home and Garden Television* network again. I'm not surprised he punked out on me. X is a big, tough dude, but he turns into a softy when Lisa comes around. Sometimes I can't believe the stuff he does for her. I always heard when you're in love with someone, you don't think twice about doing things for them. I can't really relate. I've been in deep "like" before. And I've definitely been in lust—a lot, but never in love. Must be a powerful thing, if it can make a dude like X turn into silly putty. I dunno why he denies it. Well, yeah I do. He has to front for the fellas so he doesn't look like a punk. But he's crazy, crazy in love with that girl! We all know that.

A month ago, I was at the crib writing when the phone rang. When I picked up and said hello, no one responded even though I heard talking in the background. It was X and his girl. He accidentally redialed my number on his cell phone and didn't know it. She was fussing at him about something. I mean she was going off! All he kept saying was, 'yes baby, I'm sorry, baby; you right, honey, okay, love...' I tried to keep from laughing, but it was too hilarious! X stands six-three, two hundred and sixty-five pounds, and lets a lil' ol' five-four chick run him? Man, it was so funny. He still doesn't know I heard him. I ain't gonna tell him either. I ain't gonna do my dawg like that! One day that might be me...nah, I don't think so!

At least I don't have to wait around the house anymore. I don't feel like doing too much of anything at this point and I ain't gonna roll out by myself. Sometimes rolling alone ain't no thing, I've had some wild stuff pop off when I was alone, but tonight ain't the night for that. I'ma go ahead and call this Anesia chick, see if I can swing by her spot.

I make the conversation short. All I need to find out is where she lives and if I can come through. She says she owns a condo down in Buckhead. I like women who have it together—the less they expect from me! No matter how hard I try, I still can't remember meeting this chick. That's not like me. My memory is usually pretty good. But I drunk a lil' too much that night.

"I'm leaving in five minutes; don't start the party without me!" I hang up and hit the road.

▼

Her directions are horrible, but eventually I find the place and it's laid out! The entrance has all these lil' waterfalls, fountains, and flowers everywhere. A long winding cobblestone road leads up to the condominiums. I had to check in with the officer at the guard shack first. That cat asked for my name, license plate number, who I was going to see, what address, and all that. I thought the man was gonna ask for my social security number next.

Anesia's building sits way in the back next to the pool and the gazebo. She's putting out some crazy dough to live in this joint. *I sure know how to pick'em,* I think to myself. I dial the number on the call box and she buzzes me in. I'm sharp. Have on my brand new cologne and lucky boxers. Feeling good, I start humming Marvin Gaye's *Let's Get It On.* I ring the doorbell, still singing. The door opens. ZWERRRRPPP! The music stops—cold! It's her roommate. She gets me outta the mood. She's short and chunky with more chins than a Chinese phone book—straight up, no joke! I smile anyway.

"Hello, I'm Leron, I'm here to see Anesia." I tilt my head to the left when I talk. I just can't look at her straight on. If she has a man, he probably takes her to work just to keep from kissing her goodbye.

"Leron, stop playing, you're so silly!"

"Huh?" I reply, confused like crazy.

"Come in." She takes my hand, leading me to the living room. Then it hits me. This chick ain't her roommate. This chick is Anesia? "Did you find the place okay? I'm not real good at giving directions," she says. I'm still in shock, waiting for some old white guy to jump outta the closet and yell, "Surprise you're on television, see the cameras?" Seems like hours pass. No old white guy. No cameras. I hear her talking to me, but I don't. "Leron? Did y—"

"Oh uh, yeah, no problem, you gave great directions." I thought this girl was gonna be *somewhat* decent. This isn't like me. I usually give girls like her a fake number. I must've been too tipsy and gave her the real one. I'm trying to remember. I dunno what happened. After all those drinks in a really dark club, every chick probably looked half-tempting—even this one. Man, I really slipped this time. It won't happen again, believe that.

We talk for a while. I crack some jokes. She giggles. We talk a lil' more. I crack more jokes. She giggles. She's cool and everything—has nice personality— I'm just not attracted to her that's all.

"Do you want some more to drink, boo?" She asks, trying her best to sound sexy. I figure I can at least get some free liquor out of this.

"Yeah, that'd be cool."

"Help yourself, I'm going to the room. You can come in when you're finished." *I know she doesn't think that we...I know she doesn't believe that I*—thoughts race through my head at internet speed. I pour another drink. This time I drink it fast to keep my buzz going. Whoa. I gotta really think about this one.

The liquor starts talking to me with a Hispanic accent—I swear! "Mira, primo! It's late. You're tired and I know you don't feel like drivin' fifty miles back to Duluth. And you got on the lucky boxers, man— you can't jinx them—you gotta keep the streak alive."

I pour another drink—down it in two gulps and head down the hall. Peeping through the cracked door, I sway inside. "Knock, knock," I say in a tipsy kiddy voice, looking lost and outta place. She motions me closer with her chubby index finger. "Beauty is only a light switch away," Spurt once told me. I take a deep breath, sigh, and turn out the light. I think about how I shoulda went to Tierra's crib.

Maybe I coulda put some duct tape over her mouth to shut her up—
everything woulda been perfect then. But I'm not there. I'm here. But
nobody has to know.

5

7:10 a.m. Saturday morning, landscapers trimming shrubs outside my window wake me up—and a brother was sleeping good too! I look around the room and notice my comforter, pillows, and stuffed puppy on the floor. The sheet balled up at the end of the bed makes it look like a wrestling match took place in here. Actually, one did. I'm not sure if it's 'cause of that Anesia girl, or the microwave burrito I ate after sneaking outta her crib before dawn, but I just had a nightmare. It took place in my old neighborhood in New Hampshire. I was in an abandoned building. Rotting wood and rusty nails lay scattered on the ground. Shattered glass crackled underneath my feet each step I took. A thick musty mist made it hard to see and even more difficult to breathe.

I heard the voices of a man and a woman. I walked closer and saw two unfamiliar people passionately kissing and embracing. The woman wore a long flowing white dress and appeared to be glowing. But the man was filthy; soot covered his face and clothes. When they noticed me, the woman jumped away as if hiding something.

"He attacked me, he attacked me," she screamed, pointing frantically. The man just stood emotionless. I launched at him and we fought. Holding nothing back, I hit him hard as I could, as many times as I could. A mad fury seized my body; adrenaline took charge. But he laughed with every blow; my punches had no affect.

The woman watched.

With throbbing fists, numb and blood-covered, I fought harder. My breathing turned to gasping. While I bent over struggling for air, he chuckled and said, "Is that all you have?"

Again, I tackled him. We fell to the ground as I ferociously pounded his face. Unable to punch anymore, I kicked him—repeatedly—but he had no bruises or marks. Nothing. The lopsided duel seemed to last millenniums. Finally exhausted, aching, and worn, I fell to my knees reaching for the woman. She glided passed me into the man's arms. All my fighting was in vain.

He looked down at me and said, "No matter what you do, she'll always come back." That's all I remember.

A second dream immediately followed. The setting was a village or someplace. I can't remember too many details but I do recall one scene.

In the street, a group of men assaulted a young woman. Pulling at her clothing, they taunted her like hyenas circling wounded prey. Villagers walked by, but no one dared to help. Suddenly, I swooped down from the sky, snatched her and took flight. I held her trembling body cradled in my arms. She was so cold and frigid. We ascended further and further. Up. Higher. I flew closer and closer towards the sun until her pale brown flesh grew lively. Watching life trickle into her fragile body, I fell in love just holding her.

The landscapers have moved to the next building. Maybe now I can finish sleeping in peace. A few minutes after putting my pillows in place and straightening the sheets, the phone rings.

"Hello!"

"Good morning, boo," Anesia says. "What are you doing?" It's seven-something in the morning. What does this chick think I'm doing? I wish I could forget about her but I see she won't let me.

"I was sleeping," I purposefully yawn loud as I can.

"I'm sorry. I didn't mean to wake you."

"Don't worry about it, I'm up now."

"I was just calling to see if you made it home safe. I got up this morning and you were gone."

I shake my head. I left 'cause I didn't wanna wake up with her lying next to me. Ugliness is ten times greater in the morning! "Oh, I had a lot to do today, I wanted to be home so I could get an early start."

"Okay, boo. Well thanks for last night. I haven't felt that good in a while." Now she's thanking me? At least no one can say I never gave to charity, I should get a tax break for this. "Why don't you stop by tonight?" she asks.

"I dunno, I told you I'm gonna be really busy today."

"Well, come by when you're done with all your stuff."

"I'm gonna be dead tired, I won't be much fun."

"Well, how about tomorrow night?" I guess I was *too* good last night. She won't accept the word 'no.'

"I dunno, we'll see. I'll call you."

"You promise?"

I don't make too many promises to anyone, but I have to tell her something. She won't quit. I feel like a chicken bone and she's an ugly pit bull. "...Yeah, girl."

"Okay, boo, I'll be waiting to hear from you, talk to you later."

What have I done? I've created a monster for real! I try going back to sleep but I can't—I give up—I gotta get ready for work in an hour anyway. Usually, I don't work on Saturdays but they were backed up so I'm helping out this one time.

▼

I've been feeling sluggish all day. That's how I get when I don't get my rest. I thought it would've worn off by now but at least I'm going home soon. It's almost four o'clock and the sun is still shining super-hot like it's mad at somebody. Ain't no wind blowing either and that makes it even worse—feels like a hundred and ten degrees. Just my luck, the company van's air conditioner isn't working. Everybody knows having no air conditioner in the middle of an Atlanta summer is murderous!

I'm on the way to my last service call in Dunwoody. This neighborhood looks like it's straight from some family TV show. People are walking their dogs, jogging, or packing up their garage sales. The houses are close together and most have brick mailboxes, fences, and sprinkler systems. Pulling into a cul-de-sac, I ease next to my customer's home. I walk up the gardenia-lined walkway and ring the doorbell. When the door opens, I put on my 'happy to be here smile.'

"Hello, I'm here to inst—wait a minute, *you're* Michelle Barkley?" I look at my clipboard.

"The woman who fell from heaven!" she says, smiling.

"Right!"

"And you're Leroy?"

"Leron."

"Sorry. Well, come on in."

"Thanks. Whew, it feels good in here. It's a scorcher today."

"That's Hotlanta for you. Have a seat. Would you like something to drink, water, tea, orange juice?"

"Water is fine." I sit on a black leather couch, noticing several glass tables covered with lil' ceramic animals, and two halogen lamps standing on the sides of her black oak entertainment center. The whole crib is spacious with a garden-style design. But I pay extra attention to her walking to the kitchen. Her auburn highlighted hair bounces with each stride. She's wearing a dark rose-colored blouse and a short black skirt, exposing her smooth slender legs. She has the build of a classical cello and I wanna play her. "I tell ya, it's definitely a small world after all," I say, sipping my ice-cold water.

"It sure is. I thought you did maintenance work in my office building."

"Oh, no. I was repairing an alarm system on the fifth floor. That's my job, to make people feel safe and secure."

"Hmm, I'll keep that in mind," she says, grinning.

I don't wanna read too deep into the comment. I've gotten burned many times for jumping to conclusions and assuming things. This time I'ma let things happen naturally.

"...Ah, let me tell you about this system. First of all, it's top of the line, you're really getting your money's worth. Our alarm receiving center monitors your home twenty-four hours a day for burglaries, electrical failures, personal attacks, fires, carbon dioxide poisoning and even medical emergencies."

"It does all that?"

"Yes, ma'am." *But I can do more,* I snicker to myself. "Are you married, do you have any kids, Ms. Barkley?" She pauses with a 'what does that have to with anything' expression. "I asked because our system is user-friendly for families." Actually, I asked because I don't want any complications but she doesn't have to know all that. "...The motion detectors are programmed to ignore small things like kids, pets—things like that—it keeps false alarms to a minimum."

Relaxing her face she answers, "Oh, okay. No, I'm not married and I don't have children or pets."

I nod and glance at the ring on her finger. It must be an engagement ring. "So this is your house all by yourself?"

"Yep, all mine!"

"That's good in a woman," I nod my head. "I admire your independence." The air grows stale for a split second. I change the subject fast. "Let me tell you another nice feature about the system. Do you have a cell phone with text messaging capabilities?"

"Yes"

"That's good because if an intruder enters your home while you're gone, the system sends a signal to the alarm receiving center which notifies the police and automatically pages you too."

"Wow! Technology is something else!"

"Yeah, it is. Oh, I almost forgot to mention we're installation quality certified by the National Burglar & Fire Alarm Association."

"What's that?"

I'm so busy looking at her that I almost forget to answer. She looks so good I can hardly think. "Oh, it's a...*uh*...a regulatory organization that makes sure we stick to certain standards—they're kinda like the policemen of the alarm system industry. I'll go ahead and get started. If you have any questions," *like what turns me on*, I laugh to myself, "please ask."

I head to the foyer to mount the alarm control panel while she sits and watches television. I can't help noticing her honey-kissed, caramel skin melting on the plush leather sofa.

The phone rings once she settles.

"Hello? I'm fine," she says, dryly. I'm eavesdropping on the conversation. It must be her man. She's talking about how she's being taken for granted and deserves better. They fuss back and forth a few minutes. I keep listening. "Greg, I'm tired, not now! We'll talk about it later; the security system man is here, okay? Bye." I jump back to work. She turns the television off and sits quietly while I finish installing the console.

"Um, excuse me Ms. Barkley?" I don't wanna disturb her but I gotta do my job. "Uh, I-I finished installing your control panel, there's a few more things I need to tell you." She's spaced out. I don't think she heard me. Ms. Bark—?"

"...Michelle. You can call me Michelle." She forces a smile.

"Okay, Michelle," I smile back. "Before I install the external sounder, door contacts, and motion detectors, I need to—" Rubbing the back of my neck, I stop. She isn't even listening. "If this isn't a good time, I can come back. But I won't be in this area again for a few days."

"That would be best. I'm sorry, I just wouldn't pay too much attention right now."

"Okay, then." When I look in her eyes, they speak to me. But I can't decipher them. It feels like she wants to say more. "Here's my card, if you can't reach me at the office, try me here," I say, scribbling my home number on the back. "Call me if you wanna talk...about the security system."

"Okay."

I follow her to the front door. "Well, I hope you feel better...Michelle. Remember, smiling uses less facial muscles than frowning," I joke in a childish voice. She smiles again, this time it's more convincing.

▼

After leaving Michelle's, I stop home to change into my basketball gear, then I head out to pick up Spurt from his ex girl's house. Spurt is one of the best mechanics in town but *his* car never runs right. I never understood that. Then again, I've seen plenty of barbers and beauticians with nappy heads!

Him and Meka have been messing with each other since sophomore year in high school. They'd go together for a few months, then break up a few months, make up, and begin the routine all over again. He slipped up and got her pregnant our junior year. I remember when his son was born. Meka went into labor at three o'clock in the morning. Me and the guys sat in that cold, stale-smelling waiting room for nine hours. Nine whole hours! Spurt acted macho throughout Meka's whole pregnancy and then he almost fainted in the delivery room. I still laugh every time I think about it. When he finally came outta the delivery room, he smiled so hard I thought his face was stuck. His voice crackled when he shouted, "It's a boy! It's a boy. I gotta son!" Huddling around him, me and the guys celebrated, cheered, and gave each other high-fives. I was overflowed with joy; I was so happy for him. Meka put him through eight and half months of stress, drama, threats—you name it. Even though both of them were young, scared, and broke, they stuck it out. They're not going together anymore, but a lot of times they act like they are. They fuss and fight through the week and when the weekend comes, they have sex like wild rabbits in heat. Let Spurt tell it, he only messes with her 'cause they have a son together. But I think there's more to it than that. Meka is convenient and he knows she'll always be around.

I turn on to Meka's street, maneuvering around three barefoot kids running around chasing a mangy dog. On the corner, a group of old men sit under a big oak tree, smoking and playing cards. I wave to them, pull next to Meka's duplex, and honk the horn. I don't like going inside her house 'cause it always smells like fried bologna and feet. And she never runs the air conditioner—ever! In the middle of the summer in HOTlanta, she sits in there under a broken ceiling fan, burning up! I dunno how she stands it.

Spurt skips out cursing and complaining. Meka runs after him with a curling iron. She's a thick girl, real solid. Spurt loves them big girls.

"What up, dawg?" He hops in the car to avoid Meka.

"What up, man? Hey, Me-me," I yell out the window, trying to keep from laughing. She's wearing a red Braves T-shirt and some cut-off hot pink shorts. Half of her head is purple highlighted braids, the other half is loose and thick, hasn't been braided yet. She waves at me and waves the curling iron at Spurt.

"Don't think you comin' back here tonight. You ain't comin' back over here. I'm tired of you, Spurt. You hear me? I'm tired!"

Sucking his teeth, he ignores her. "Let's ride, man." He ain't worried; he knows she'll be calling him to come spend the night later.

"She got you running?" I laugh.

"I ain't worried 'bout her."

Meka screams as I pull off. "I mean it Spurt! Don't come back, I mean it!"

The further I drive, the smaller she appears in the rear view mirror. All I can see now is a hot pink blur. "What's that all about, man?"

"What you think? You know how it is. It's 'bout time I get some new booty on duty. I might have to get me one of 'dem Leron type broads. This drama gotta go." Spurt sounds more frustrated than usual. I can't believe he thinks he can get the type of chicks I get. He can't be serious. "What'd you end up doing last night, you and X went back out, right?" He asks.

"Man, I ain't go nowhere with X, he stayed home. Lisa had him on lockdown. But this bombshell chick I met at the Garden called; she was like, 'come through,' so I did."

"Oh yeah?"

"Yeah, man." She gotta condo out in Buckhead. This chick is blazin.' She got her own money, a tight crib, and a body outta this world!" What am I supposed to say? I ain't gonna tell him the chick reminds me of a creature from *Star Wars*. I have a reputation to keep.

"Yeah, yeah!" Spurt answers excitedly. "Rich and fine! You handled that?"

"C'mon now," I jab his shoulder. "Who you talking to, man? She blowin' up my phone trying to get me to come back!"

"I need to roll with you more often, I wanna meet a broad like that!"

"You ain't ready, man. You ain't ready," I kid him, trying not to chuckle. I remember once he told me I dunno how to pick women. And that I need to stop going after them 'high-class, intelligent broads and get a real shorty, a simple one—easy to please.' And now he's telling me this?

"What you mean I ain't ready? I can spit game to any chick. It don't matter."

"Your game ain't tight enough, these chicks outta your league."

"What? Outta my league? Man, please! Look here, I bet you I pull one by the end of the summer. I got fifty dollars on it." He sounds offended but I'm just having fun with him. He's taking it serious.

I laugh. "I don't wanna take your money."

"A hundred dollars then! I'll use yo money to help fix my car."

"I was just playing with you, Spurt."

He fans the air as if pushing my words aside. "You just don't wanna lose yo money, that's all.

"Are you serious?"

"As a heart attack."

"All right then, a hundred dollars."

"True, it's on now, baby boy!"

6

I feel bad at how rude I was to Leron, the security system man. He caught me at a bad time. I was actually in a good mood until Greg called me. I used to feel so special and desired when we talked. But now I feel sick and abandoned. Why do the ones you love the most hurt you the worst? That's only one of the five thousand questions swirling in my head. I know Greg truly loves me, but it doesn't feel like the unconditional, lifetime commitment love he used to have.

In our brief phone conversation, he said it was urgent that we talk. That's fine, because I need to tell him some things too. He tried giving me a long speech about our relationship and where he felt it was heading, etc., etc. I stopped him. I wasn't in the right mindset and Leron was installing my new alarm system. Reluctantly, he agreed to talk later tonight over dinner. This time I'm not breaking my neck getting ready; I'm taking my sweet little time. I want to purposely show up late. I know it's spiteful, but I don't want to miss the end of *The Golden Girls*.

I arrive a quarter after seven o'clock—fifteen minutes late. It's not too crowded yet but the dinner crowd is slowly filing in. It will start getting packed around eight thirty or so. I know the restaurant well. I used to love this place: the antique memorabilia on the walls, the friendly staff, the ice cream floats. Greg and I ate here almost every week when we first began dating. But it has lost its appeal. It hasn't changed that much but I have.

I walk down the aisle and see Greg sitting in a corner booth, looking out the window, impatiently tapping on the table. He hates when I'm late. I saw that episode of *The Golden Girls* three times already but I watched it again. With a sincere expression, I take a seat. "Hi, baby, sorry I'm late."

Greg does a bad job of hiding the frustrated look on his face. "...It's okay. But I was getting worried for a min—"

A waitress steps to the table. "Hello, my name is Cindy, I'll be your server today. Can I start you off with something to drink?"

"I'll have a water with lemon, please."

"And you sir?"

"Cranberry juice."

"So how've you been, baby? I missed you." He strokes my hand with his thumb. Whatever he has to say is eating him up inside.

"Fine," I reply knowing he hates one-word answers.

"Are you feeling okay?"

"Yes," I tell him, barely opening my mouth. I want him to hurry up and say whatever he has to say. I'll do the same and we'll be done with it. Communicating is not his strong point. Often he'll hold things in for months and months, little things. By the time he gets around to talking, I've forgotten the whole thing—which annoys him even more. I like dealing with conflict while it's fresh, settling it, and moving on. But everyone has their own ways of handling things I guess. "So what's on your mind, Greg? What did you want to talk about?"

He adjusts his glasses and sighs. Fiddling with my fingers to ease his tension, his lips part, "Michelle, I know things have been rough lately. I've been really stressed. I've been unfair to you and that's not right…"

"Here are your drinks, let me know when you're ready to order," the waitress interrupts then leaves.

Greg continues, "I wish I was eloquent enough to express how I feel about you. They say actions speak louder than words, crazy as I've been acting, you'd think I didn't love you at all…" I reassure him by smiling. He's adorable when he struggles to express his feelings. Like a little kid he gets antsy and never holds much eye contact—but he's sincere. "I can make everything up to you, if you let me."

"Greg, I—"

"From now on, everything is about you—all about you, baby. I can't imagine being without you. I don't know what I'd do if I couldn't see your smile, stroke your hair, hear your sweet voice in my ears…"

I've never heard him express his feelings this way, but it doesn't change how I feel—it just makes it harder. "Greg, I've been thinking about things. At first, I thought your job was the cause of our problems. But I've realized that we were growing apart long before you started this project."

"What do you mean? We've been great together. You even agreed to be my wife. Now you're saying we're growing apart?"

"What I'm saying is—"

"We've just hit a little snag, baby, that's all. It's completely natural—nothing we can't work out."

I wait for him to finish before speaking my mind. "I just think maybe we moved too fast. Maybe we should slow down, take some time to see if this is what we really want."

"Of course this is what we want! I love you, and you love me—right?"

I huff, "Yes but—"

"Then what else do we need?"

"Time."

"Time?"

"We need time, at least I do." I sip some water to moisten my throat, "Time to reevaluate myself—and us."

Agitated, he puts his face in his hands, then stares out the window, then at me. "...Remember when you used to work at that boutique in the mall? That day I came in you asked if I needed help finding something. When you smiled at me, I felt warm inside. You told me how you had worked there a few months and that it was a nice place; but you could never afford anything in there. Do you remember that?"

"...Yes." I begin fluttering inside. I remember perfectly.

Placing both hands on mine, he continues, "I told you I was looking for something nice for a friend—you helped me pick out this beautiful sundress. Remember after I bought it, you folded it neatly and bagged it? I looked into your deep brown eyes and said keep it.

You told me you never felt that special before. You said that was the nicest thing anyone had ever done for you."

"It was. But...you don't do things like that anymore, baby. Yes, you buy me nice things, but it's the little things that matter the most to me. I don't feel so special anymore."

"What do you mean? I go out of my way to make you feel special. I still do those things—nothing's changed."

"No you don't, Greg."

"Yes, I do."

"No you—" I stop myself. He honestly thinks nothing has changed? "When was the last time you gave me a card and flowers just because?"

"I—"

"What about those sweet little notes you used to leave on my car every once and a while?"

"Well, I—"

I pause. "...When was the last time we made love, Greg?"

His eyes widen as he sits straight up against the back of the seat. "Baby, come on I—"

"When? See what I mean?" I slide the engagement ring off my finger.

"W-What are you doing?"

"I want you to keep this." I put the ring in his hand and close it tight. "Baby, I'm not saying I don't want to marry you, I'm just saying we need to take some time off. I just wouldn't feel comfortable wearing this right now."

"Don't do this. I need you Michelle. I need your support now more than ever. This just isn't a good time to start pulling stunts like th—"

"It's better this way, Greg. It may not seem that way now, but later down the line you'll realize it." I stand up from the table. "I still love you, I just feel this is the right thing to do." When I kiss his forehead, he closes his eyes, saying nothing. I kiss his cheek and then began to walk towards the exit. I want to turn around but for once, I'm not going to be a slave to my emotions. I continue walking down the aisle and out the door.

▼

There isn't one decent song on the radio. Every station has some woman wailing about her heart being broken—I don't want to hear that. I need something uplifting. I put in Michael Jackson's *Off the Wall. Don't Stop* dances out of the speakers.

...Don't stop til' you get enough, he sings to me. The pain in my head evaporates with each beat of the bass line. *...Keep on...don't stop until you get enough...*

"Owww! Sing it Michael," I scream as if he can hear me. "Go ahead!" Working my shoulders and tapping my fingers on the wheel, I sing along. The bass echoes off the windows. I'm grooving so hard I miss my exit but I'm not bothering to turn around. I drive and drive: around I-285, down to the Georgia 400, across to I-75, and through downtown. The Olympic Flame tower appears higher; the Varsity sign downtown shines brighter; and the Fox Theater seems more majestic. I see so many things. Many I've seen before but now I see them differently.

Hours later, I pull into the garage and sit while the last song plays. I feel rejuvenated. My muscles are loose with an invincible mellowness. Grabbing my purse, I go inside still singing off-key— Michael doesn't care. After throwing my keys on the table, I notice Leron's business card. I hold it in my hand and read the bold printed letters: Leron King, Security Systems Technician. *Smiling uses less facial muscles than frowning,* his words ring in my head. I smile. I just might give him a call so we can talk...about my security system.

7

The park has two basketball courts: A and B. A court is for the real ballers, those that really know how to play. B court is for everyone else. Me and the fellas play on A court. We're all decent shooters except for Dave. He can't shoot an arrow in the sky without missing but he plays good defense. I look forward to our Sunday evening games 'cause it's the only day all five of us can play together. We run three games and afterwards, sit around talking for a few minutes before leaving then I dropped Spurt off at his crib. Soon as I reached my apartment, I slipped outta my sweaty Atlanta Hawks jersey, stretched, and headed straight to the shower. Afterwards, I ate a baked ziti frozen dinner at my desk.

That's where I've been for a while, looking at this blank screen trying to think of something to write. I have a serious case of writer's block. I shoulda quit already. I write better late at night and it's only nine o'clock. I need inspiration, something to spark some creativity. Television time. I stretch across the living room sofa and begin flipping through channels.

"...Popeye, I brought you on the show to tell you I've been sleeping with your bro—"

"...Two store clerks shot and killed at an East Point gas sta—"

"...I made thousands of dollars placing tiny classified ads from my one bedroom apart—"

"...Are secrets being kept from you? Call me now for your free psychic read—"

"...Order right now and receive this beautiful gold plated neck—"

"...White grubs are the larvae of Scarab beetles. There are more than twenty species of—"

So much for inspiration! All these channels and I can't find anything worth watching. Sitting back in front of the computer, I log online to check my email—see what kinda of crazy forwards my boy Joe from back home sent—he never writes actual messages.

I knew it. Three messages from Joe—all forwards. Since I'm bored, I'll actually read them this time. In the middle of the second one, an instant message pops on the screen.

Nhprincess: <Hey handsome, are you busy? I'm stressed. I need to talk>

LeronK: <Fantastic Femia! What's wrong?>

Nhprincess: <Are you sure you want me to bore you with my problems?>

LeronK: <Why not? You bore me with everything else! Just joking! Haha.>

Nhprincess: <Funny. I'm calling you in five minutes.>

Fantastic Femia. I call her that because she always has a million things going on. She loves challenges, but often takes on more than she can handle. Balancing graduate school, work, clubs, associations, community service, and church choir is a lot for anybody—even her. I often tease about her 'save-the-world' mentality; constantly putting her needs aside to help others. But she's helped me a lot too, so I don't hesitate when she needs me.

Her voice sounds full of anticipation when she says "hello."

To lighten the mood, I answer in a raspy preacher's voice. "Hey, sister, this is the Reverend Love A. Lot, can I lay my hands on you?"

She laughs hysterically. "Ron, you're a real nut, you know that? The Reverend Love A. Lot, you crack me up!"

"So what's up with you, girl?"

"I am so stressed right now! I have three midterms to study for and a twelve-page paper due—all next week."

My call-waiting beeps, I ignore it. "Twelve-page paper? You're a Math major, you shouldn't have to *write* anything!"

"I know! Speaking of writing, how's your book coming?"

"Well, I can see the light at the end of the tunnel, but I'm kinda losing interest."

"You've come this far, don't quit now! I would read what you have so far, but I just don't have time with all these tests and everything."

"Oh, don't worry about it, you need to focus on school."

"Yeah, I'm really worried about Vector Differential Calculus."

"Who, what, what?"

"Vector Differential Calculus. I need to ace it to raise my average."

"That sounds like some kinda foot fungus or something!"

"You're so nasty!"

"Just do what I would do. Sit by some Asian dude and copy him."

"Yeah, that sounds like something *you'd* do—but I don't cheat!"

"Go talk to the professor if you have to. If that doesn't work, show him some leg!"

"He's gay."

"Oh."

"But maybe you could show him yours?"

"Ha, funny. Hey, you didn't finish telling me why you and your man broke up." Femia gets quiet before saying her and her ex boyfriend didn't seem right for each other; and she doesn't know how they lasted this long. She had certain goals in life she wanted to achieve, and he wasn't trying to do anything. They were on two separate paths. I ask her why it took whole year to figure that out. She sighs and says she kinda felt that way midway through the relationship but was used to having him around and didn't want to be alone. "You wouldn't understand, Ron." She sighs, "Whenever you get lonely you just call one of your hoochies and—"

"Hoochies? I only date wholesome girls!" My call-waiting beeps again just as I'm about to defend myself. "Hey, hold on a sec, I got somebody on the other line." I click over and hear a familiar voice.

"Hey, boo? You forgot all about me, didn't you?" It's Anesia, the pit bull.

"Nah, baby girl, I didn't forget. I'ma call you in about ten or fifteen minutes. I'm on long distance with my boy from back home."

"Okay, I'll be here. Don't make me wait to long."

"Was that one of your *wholesome* hoochies?" Femia asks when I click back over.

"No. That was my man Spurt. He needs a ride to work in the

morning."

Since we are on the topic of my women, Femia asks me if anything interesting is going on 'cause usually I have something juicy to say. That's when I tell her about me and Michelle bumping into each other twice; and that she's engaged but the relationship is rocky. Femia almost chokes on my words. Rocky relationship or not, she thinks I should leave Michelle alone.

"There are plenty of nice *single* women out there," she says.

"Yeah, I know. But I was picking up these vibes from her and—"

"Are you sure that wasn't gas?"

"Stick to math, comedy ain't your thing."

"Shut up!"

"Well, I gotta go back and finish installing her security system so maybe I'll get to know her a lil' better."

"Whatever you do, just take it slow. Don't force anything," she says. After preaching a few more minutes, Femia says she feels a lot better than she did before we talked. I tell her it's nice to talk with a girl who doesn't get on my nerves whining and complaining all the time. She tells me how sweet that was then asks if I'm coming to her graduation.

"I missed your last one but I ain't missing this one if I can help it."

"Yeah, you better come if you know what's good for you!" she jokes.

After we hang up, I shake my head. That girl's just as crazy as me.

8

I left work early 'cause I wasn't feeling too good. Mondays are always slow anyway; no one will even miss a brother. All I need is some headache powder, a few hours of sleep and I'll be cool. I jump in bed soon as I get home, shoes on and all. My pillow gladly welcomes my heavy head. After shifting several times, I find a nice position, yawn, and doze off. My long weekend still has me beat. I can even hear myself snoring and I don't snore unless I'm dead tired. It feels so good to get some rest. Ain't nothing like a good carefree nap.

Strangely, thirty-five minutes later, my alarm clock goes off. I ignore it, roll over and bury my head back on the pillow. Finally, it stops. Ten minutes later, it goes off again. I swing at the snooze button but the noise continues. Suddenly, I realize it's the phone—not my clock. People are always calling me when I'm sleeping good. Whoever it is keeps calling and hanging up just before voicemail can answer. Completely outta the sleep groove, I snatch the phone.

"Hello?"

"Why didn't you call me back? You promised you would call me back. You knew I was wait—"

"Who is this?" I ask, looking at my caller ID. Private Number.

"Don't play dumb with me, who do you think it is?" It was a familiar female voice but I wasn't about to just start calling out names—that's crazy!

"Look," I scratch the corner of my mouth, "I don't have time for games—who is this?"

"It's Anesia! What, do you have so many women you can't even tell their voices apart?"

My equilibrium is still off, and her shrill tone is killing my ears. "Can you please lower your voice?"

"Nope! I'm loud because I'm pissed. Why didn't you call me back last night?"

"Sorry, I forgot."

"Forgot? Yeah, I bet y—"

"How did you know I was home?"

"I called your job and they told me you left for the day—"

"You called my j—how did you get my work num—?"

She ignores me and says, "If you didn't want to come over, I would've understood. But don't make promises you can't k—"

"Anesia, I said I was sorry. I forgot, okay?" I know she can hear the irritation in my voice. I'm getting defensive. I'm tired and my stomach is growling. "Are you done? I'm really not up for this right now."

"I don't need this Leron," she says, lowering her voice a lil'. "I—"

"Hold one sec, I gotta another call." I'm lying. Ain't nobody on the other line, I'm just clicking over to give my ear a break. Hopefully she'll hang up. "Okay, I'm back," I say, switching the phone to the other ear, "Hello? Hellooooo?" Good, it worked. Ready to finish napping, I fluff my pillow.

The phone rings. Private Number. But I know it's the pit bull.

"You had me on hold too long, so I hung up. I don't like waiting."

"My bad," I reply, hoping that maybe we can discuss this like adults.

"Leron, I just thought you were a little more considerate than this." She's really making a big deal about this—a *real* big deal. *Beep...Beep...Beep*, the warning signals sound in my head. She's definitely a clinging type chick, latches on to any guy giving her a lil' attention. I ain't the one! I don't interrupt her, though 'cause I'm *considerate*. "...We had a lot of fun and I thought you were interested in me," she says.

"I *am* considerate, and we *did* have fun. You're a very nice girl but—"

"Nice girl? Nice? How many times have I heard that line?"

"Well, you are and you have a great personal—"

"Teddy bears are—*nice*. Little puppies are—*nice*..." A picture of a pit bull flashes in my head. "What does *nice* mean?" Her voice sharpens. "Nice enough to sleep with, but not for a relationship?"

Relationship? She just said relationship! That triggers my warning sirens again. Computerized voices reverberate within me: *Warning. Warning. Relationship does not compute. Relationship does not compute!* I zone out for a split second; somehow, I manage to form a complete sentence. "A relationship? Girl, I hardly know you, let alone want to have a—"

"That didn't stop you from coming in my room Friday night, did it?" She has a good point and I can't think of much to say.

"Girl, you crazy!" That's my universal response when I can't think of anything better. I take a deep breath and exhale hard. I know I probably shoulda called her, but this outburst is unnecessary. "Can we talk about this a lil' later, I'm tired and—"

"I DON'T WANT TO TALK LATER! I want to talk now," she screams like she just hugged a porcupine. "I'm so sick of men treating me like I'm some towel they can just use and throw on the floor—"

"Whoa, hold up! I ain't force you to do anything! You're a grown woman, everything you did, you wanted—"

"I don't deserve this. I finally meet a guy who actually talks and listens to what I have to say...and he ends up being a dog just like the others!"

"Hey, obviously some dude hurt you, but I'm not that man. Don't blow up at me!"

"...You don't want to see me anymore so just say it."

"We can be friends—"

"Don't give me that, be a man, just tell me the truth. Say it!"

"Girl, stop act—"

"Go ahead..."

"Why are you being s—"

"SAY IT, sissy!"

"FINE! I don't wanna see you. Happy now?"

"DOG!"

"No, you the dog, you ugly lil' pit b—" She hangs up.

"Ruff, ruff, dumb trick!" I slam the phone into its cradle and lean against the headboard, steaming. The phone rings again. Private number.

"WHAT?"

"YO MAMA!" Anesia yells and hangs up.

How childish can you get? I don't understand how all this happened. I mean, I just met the chick and she's trippin' already. I knew I shoulda just stayed home Friday. I woulda had one less headache.

The phone rings again. Private number. This time I answer with a serious attitude.

"DON'T CALL MY HOUSE ANYMORE, TRICK!"

There's a brief pause before anyone speaks. "...Excuse me? I think I dialed the wrong number," says a plush velvet female voice. Her tone and inflection are so soothing and mellow my temper fades instantaneously. "I was calling for Leron King..."

"Oh, uh, this is Leron." I'm glad it wasn't my mother!

"Hello, Leron, this is Michelle. Michelle Barkley. You installed a security system for me last week."

"Michelle! Hey, how are you?"

"I'm fine. For a minute I thought I dialed the wrong number."

"Oh, sorry about that; just a prank caller playing jokes—what can I do for you?"

"Well, I was wondering what day you planned on finishing my system. I want to make sure I'm home."

Recognizing a golden opportunity, I ask, "How about today? I'm not too busy right now." *Besides, I wanna get back over there as soon as possible,* I say to myself.

"Today? Oh, um, I don't know. I'm at the office..."

"Oh, well then how about Thur—"

"But I can be home in forty minutes. Is that okay?"

Perfect! I think to myself. "Hmmm," I pause as if thinking deeply, "I guess that's fine." I didn't wanna sound too anxious. This is great! Suddenly, my headache has magically disappeared.

▼

I make it to Michelle's house in no time and she answers the door with a smile. "Come on in," she motions me to the living room. "Are you in a rush?"

"No, actually I'm in no hurry at all. Today has been a light day."

"Well, good. Have a seat. Relax, let's chat a minute before you start." I take a seat at the end of the sofa. Michelle sits next to me in a loveseat. "I want to apologize for not letting you finish last week. I just needed some time alone."

"Oh, I understand. It's no big deal."

She smiles and asks, "How was your weekend?"

"I didn't do anything too exciting. I gotta lot of writing done, though."

"You write?"

"Yeah, but not as much as I used to. But I'm getting back into it. I'm writing a novel now."

"Really?" She leans forward, eyes lighting up like two roman candles. "How exciting. What's it about if you don't mind me asking?"

"Well, I'm still developing the idea, but so far it's about a player who finally realizes what women truly want in a man."

"Now that sounds *very* interesting. Is this an autobiography? Let me guess, you're the player and you're writing about yourself?" She cocks her head to the side and waits for my answer.

"Oh, no. It's completely fiction. I'm no player," I tell her, making eye contact. "Players play games—I don't like games."

She pauses before speaking. Judging from her facial expression, she's satisfied with my answer. "...Well, a lot of men do. Maybe they can learn something from your book then?"

"Maybe."

"I used to write poetry, but I stopped," she sighs, leaning back in the loveseat, casually stroking her hair. "I was just too busy I guess...I wasn't that good anyway."

"You should start writing again. It's not about being good or bad; it's about expressing your feelings and emotions. Getting my thoughts on paper is therapeutic sometimes, especially, when I'm stressed."

"Hmm, I never thought of it that way. I need all the stress relief I can get! So, Mr. Big Time Writer, can I have a copy of your book when it's done?"

"No. But you can have an *autographed* copy!"

She grins.

Time steadily passes and every time I mention finishing the installation, she brushes it aside. I'm not upset about it 'cause I wanna keep talking just as much as she does. I guess we both have our reasons and motives for continuing the conversation. All I know is that finally I'm starting to make progress.

9

Grayish clouds roll across the sky, covering up the sun. The ground is already wet from last night's rain shower and it's probably gonna rain again soon, judging from the sound of thunder in the distance. The bad weather fits my mood perfectly. An hour ago, I was on my way to work when my Jeep Grand Cherokee started making weird sputtering sounds. It jerked a couple times and cut off in the center lane of Peachtree Industrial Boulevard. I must've tried to restart the thing a hundred times before finally breaking down and having it towed to the car shop where Spurt works. I've been standing in one of the garages for hours it seems, watching him fiddle around under the hood. I can't believe this. It's only 8:24 Tuesday morning and I'm already in a bad mood. Everything is just...just pissing me off: the gasoline, oil, and rubber fumes; the peeling blue paint on the shop walls; the dirty fingerprint smudges on the windows—everything is pissing me off! I keep pacing back and forth like I'm playing dodge ball or something. That's the only way I can keep my cool.

"They did what?" I ask Spurt again.

He scratches the top of his head and repeats, "Somebody poured sugar in your gas tank. You stalled 'cause your fuel pump is clogged—the whole fuel system is shot."

"Man, I don't believe this," I shake my head, "So what do I need done? Just tell me what I'm looking at."

"Well, first we gotta drop your gas tank and drain it; make sure it's completely clean," he wipes his hands on an oil-stained hand towel. "We might even have to rebuild the engine. I'ma be straight up with you, this gonna be expensive."

"This is crazy! I've only had this car six months!"

"I wish you woulda seen who did it. We coulda ruffed him up."

"Probably some lil' punk—I don't really care—I just need to get my ride fixed. How long will it take?"

Spurt closes the hood. "Should be ready by Thursday."

I sure hope so. Michelle invited me to some French café for beignets and coffee. I've never had beignets so she insisted I try them. "You sure?" I ask Spurt, looking very concerned. "I'm hooking up with this new chick Thursday night. I *need* my ride."

"Don't worry 'bout it man, I got it under control. You done met another girl?"

I lean against the car door and nod. "Yeah, I installed her system; cute light-skinned honey, real sweet. You know it was all over once I kicked game!"

"I hear you, playa, I hear you. Check this out. This fine, sophisticated shorty came in yesterday for a tune-up lookin' all sexy in her lil' business suit."

"She gave you her number?"

"What you think? Yeah, I got the digits," he grins like a kid with a full stomach, "You might be payin' me a hundred dollars pretty soon, baby boy."

"You asked for her number and she just gave it to you?"

"Man, you know I had to do a *lil'* talkin.' She wasn't trying to just gimme it, dawg. Broads wanna be chased. I keep tellin' you."

"Yeah, yeah, yeah. I'm blowed, man."

"You know how I do it; I caught eye contact then I stepped to her." He demonstrates on an imaginary girl. "I was like, 'baby, if I followed you home, would you keep me?' She started smiling." *She fell for that?* I think to myself. "I spit a lil' more game and that was that. Told you, dawg," he beats his chest. "Ain't no broad outta my league!"

"Well, I ain't paying you nothing until I meet her."

"True dat, it's all good. I'ma work my magic. You just make sure my hundred-dollar bill is crisp—I don't like wrinkled money!"

"Yeah, whatever," my voice trials off as I whip out my cell phone to call the office to let them know I'll be in late. The receptionist says a woman has been calling for me all morning but never leaves a message. I'm trying to remember if I missed any appointments, but nothing comes to mind. If it's important, she'll keep calling until she gets me.

I call X too since he works from home today. He says he'll take me to work. He sounds strange, like he's anxious to get out the house. Either Lisa or staring at that computer screen too much is probably getting to him. He makes it to the shop in twenty minutes, says a few words to Spurt, and then we hit I-75. He's unusually quiet. I thought he'd be making wise cracks about having "sugar in my tank." But he's not making any. None. No cheap shots. No low blows. Nothing. Something is obviously wrong. I ask what the deal is. He hesitates before finally opening up. He tells me how he first met Lisa. And how he knows she's the one he'll spend his life with. He talks about how he's really in love but tries to hide it around the fellas—even though we already know that much. He makes me promise not to tell the guys that he proposed last week. Of course, I'm happy for him. Shoot, they already act married, might as well make it legal.

I thought he'd be bubbling with happiness, but he isn't. While he's talking, I find out the reason why. Yesterday he found out his company is gonna lay him off in two weeks. I'm the only person that knows. Lisa doesn't even know and she has the nose of a bloodhound. He says his skills are in high demand and getting another job won't be a problem. He's more concerned about Lisa's reaction. She can be uptight sometimes, so I understand why he hasn't told her. She would be so stressed out; you'd think *she's* being laid off. I tell him to go ahead and tell her, 'cause if she finds out on her own, things will get ugly.

As we pull into the parking lot, he thanks me for listening and again makes me promise to keep quiet. He says I'm the only one outta the crew he trusts with something like this. I give him my word, thank him for the lift, and head inside. I feel like an outdated computer trying to process all this info. But I'm glad he finally proposed. They're good together. He loves giving and she loves taking. Perfect. I guess.

▼

Late Wednesday night I couldn't help worrying if Spurt would have my ride ready today or not. So, when he called me this afternoon and told me to pick it up after work, I was relieved. I'm glad I didn't have to cancel dinner with Michelle 'cause that might've given her a bad impression and I'm trying to start out on the right foot.

The café is tucked in a downtown corner off of West Peachtree. It takes me ten minutes to park and I still end up walking four blocks. At least Michelle's directions were good. The smell of flavored coffee consumes the entire café. The place is small and intimate, not many people. Glowing light from candles on the tables flicker to soft classical music playing overhead.

When Michelle sees me, she smiles and waves me to the table. She looks like she just left the beauty salon. Her slightly curled hair frames her smooth face and I can hardly tell if she's wearing make-up or not. If she is, she doesn't need it. "You found it!"

I grab a chair and sit down. "Yeah, finding it wasn't a problem, parking...well, that's another story."

"So are you ready to taste some mouth-watering beignets?"

I'm ready to taste some mouth-watering you, I joke in my head. "I sure am. I hope they're as good as you say."

"Trust me, but I'll let you judge."

"That works for me. Let's eat then!" I open the menu and see no main dishes listed. "Is this the dessert menu?" I ask.

Michelle laughs and says, "Leron, they only serve coffee, tea, hot chocolate and French pastries here."

"So you're saying they don't have food-food here? How do they stay in business?" I chuckle.

The waiter asks us what we'll be ordering. Without looking at the menu, Michelle orders beignets and French vanilla coffee. She sounds like she knows her stuff so I order the same thing.

"By the way, Michelle, you look lovely. That silk blouse looks very nice on you." *It would look even better on my bedroom floor,* I think to myself. "It really compliments your skin tone."

"Oh, this is just something I wore to work, but thanks."

"Well, I like it. It's nice. How's your security system? Is everything working okay?"

"Yes, it's working fine. And now I feel safe and secure thanks to you."

"Just doing my job lil' lady," I say, with a poor John Wayne imitation. She finds it amusing.

"How long have you been doing the security system thing?"

"Ah, about ten months or so. Before that I sold used cars but I wasn't too good at it."

"You sold cars?"

"Yeah. Hard to believe, huh?"

"Well, not really," she leans forward, resting her chin in her hand. "I find you very persuasive." The expression on her face says, 'I want you so bad, let's take it to the crib right now'...I think.

"Well, can I persuade you to let me take you out sometime?" I ask with increasing confidence.

She grins. "You can try."

The waiter returns with our food. I cautiously bite into a hot beignet not knowing what to expect. Michelle is watching me closely to see my facial expression.

"Mmm tasty, very tasty." I lick the powdered sugar from my fingers.

"I knew you would like them."

I nod my head, take a sip of coffee and ask, "So, what exactly do you do?"

She holds up her index finger signaling me to wait while she swallows. "...I'm a Senior Account Executive at an advertising agency. It has its good and bad moments, but my days there are numbered."

"What do you mean?"

"I don't want to be in advertising my entire life. What I really want to do is teach. There's a great need for teachers and I think I can help make a difference."

"If I had teachers as beautiful as you, I'd purposely get in trouble just to stay after class."

She cuts her eyes at me. "That's cute. Real cute."

I smile.

"You're a smooth-talker, Leron. Do you have a girlfriend? And does she know how much you like to sweet talk?"

I stuff the remains of a beignet into my mouth. "No. I'm single and taking applications from the right candidates."

"Uh huh. Do you have a lot of ...*candidates* applying?"

I wipe my mouth and answer, "Not qualified ones."

She leans back in the chair. "What qualifications are you looking for—no wait, let me guess: big breasts, big butt, long hair, and green eyes?"

I burst into a short laugh. "Ha! You've been watching too many music videos! I just wanna nice woman. I used to ramble off a long list of things, but I came to a realization—I'm not looking for the *perfect* woman—I'm just looking for the perfect woman for me. You?"

She breaks eye contact to sip more coffee. "What about me?"

"Well, you're not married, but I'd be shocked if you weren't seeing anyone." Of course, I know she has man. I just wanna hear the scoop from her. Plus, I see she's not wearing her ring.

"Actually, I'm engaged," she fiddles with the cup handle, slowly turning it side to side. "Greg and I have been engaged five months now."

"What a lucky guy. Why didn't you accidentally bump into me five months ago? Your timing is terrible!" We both chuckle and then I ask why she isn't wearing a ring.

The swift splash of tension skirting across the room makes her posture stiffen and eyes wander. With a constipated 'stop being nosey' expression she says, "...It's in a safe place." Then she makes a special effort to tell me she's deeply in love with this Greg guy and that they're just ironing outta few wrinkles. Unlike my man Spurt, I don't like rejection. So I need to see what I'm up against, see if I should bother. That's why I wanna make sure my chances are good before I take things any further. I clear my throat to break the awkwardness and continue my interrogation. "When's the big day?"

Holding the coffee cup to her mouth as if shielding herself from my words, she mutters, "Sometime next year, we haven't decided on a date." She pats her lips with a napkin and gives a weird look. I get the hint and change the subject to something less touchy.

"So tell me about yourself, you from Atlanta?" I ask.

"Orlando."

"What made you move?"

"My job and the fact that I always wanted to live here, it's a great city. I interviewed when I was in college. When I got the job, I moved. Are you from Atlanta?"

"No. I'm from Manchester, New Hampshire. I came here when I was eight."

"New Hampshire? You're the first person I ever met from there."

I smile. "Yeah, I hear that a lot."

"What is there to do in New Hampshire?"

"Absolutely nothing!"

We both laugh.

Before we know it, we're the only customers remaining. I got here a little after nine o'clock and it's almost 11:00 p.m., and we're still talking. We discuss everything from politics to old television shows, to fifty-year-old men still hanging in nightclubs. We aren't even aware of the time until the manager says he's closing.

"Once again I enjoyed myself, Leron," Michelle says as we're leaving the cafe. I hold the door until she passes through.

"I did too. I completely lost track of time."

"We both did. But I needed some good conversation, I'm glad you came."

We leisurely stroll to her car, trying to make the five-minute walk last an hour. Secretly, we exchange quick glances. But nothing is secret anymore. We know.

"So did I persuade you?"

She looks at me with a playful look. "Persuade me to what?"

I smile 'cause I know she knows exactly what I'm talking about. I play the game anyway. "...To let me take you out sometime."

"...You know I'm engaged and—"

"Michelle, if you were a hundred percent sure about this guy, we wouldn't even be here right now."

"Well I—"

"And if you were so in love like you told me, you'd still be wearing that ring."

"I told you that I—"

I cut her off again. "I'm not trying to replace Greg. I just wanna spend time with you; maybe a movie here, dinner there—that's all I'm asking," I place my hand on the car, trapping her between my arm and the door. "I enjoy your company and you enjoy mine, so why shouldn't we?"

Michelle looks in my eyes. Hopefully, I didn't sound too aggressive. I just wanted to make my point clear. She adjusts the handbag strap over her shoulder, smiles and says, "I told you that you're *very* persuasive. How can a woman resist those eyes?" She opens the car door and I hold it until she settles inside. "I'll call you," she says. It's still not a definite answer but I don't wanna press the issue anymore, at least not now.

She drives off waving goodbye. With my hands in my pocket, I watch her white Toyota Avalon turn the corner and disappear. I had a nice time, and the beignets were delicious, but I need some meat. I stop and get a triple cheeseburger meal on the way home.

10

I thought about Leron all the way home, when I undressed, and I'm thinking about him now as I bathe. The warm bathwater soothes my body while John Coltrane's tenor saxophone soothes my ears. All the lights are off. Two peach-scented candles sitting on the bathroom counter provide the only light I need. Closing my eyes, I sink deeper for a few more minutes of pleasure before stepping out of the tub. Suds pop and fizzle as I dry off and replay tonight in my mind. I shouldn't have stayed out so late because I have a busy day tomorrow. But it was worth it. I had a great time and I needed to get out for a change. I wonder if my hair looked okay or if Leron liked my smile. He must've known I was thinking about him because he calls as soon as I get in bed.

"Hey, it's Leron. I know it's late and I didn't call to talk long. I just wanted to make sure you made it home safe," he says, sounding genuinely concerned.

"Yes, I did. Thanks for checking on me, that's so sweet of you."

"Your alarm is set, right?"

"Yes, it's armed and ready. Just like you showed me."

He chuckles softly. "Good, I wanted to make sure everything was cool before I went to sleep. Sweet dreams, sleep well."

"Thank you, sweet dreams to you too."

I've enjoyed the couple of times Leron and I have spent together. He's funny, confident, insightful, and he keeps my attention. I feel confident and secure—like I can do anything when he's around. His energy and ambition inspires me. I felt the same way about Greg not too long ago. I've been thinking about what Leron said about Greg and me. He may have a point. Maybe I'm not deeply in love like I thought. Or maybe I was deeply in love and I'm not now? Or maybe I was never in love to begin with? Or maybe I still am and don't know it...I don't know. I just don't want to be hurt and I don't want to hurt anyone either.

▼

When the alarm clock buzzed this morning, I jumped right up without hitting the snooze button. I thought I'd be groggy, but I feel wonderful. My client meeting at 8:30 a.m. didn't last long and I made it back to the office rather early. I'm going to use the time to finally read those *urgent* emails that have sat in my inbox for days. In the middle of reading a dirty joke from Mrs. Feinstein, Ann Mason, my supervisor peeks in. She's shorter and heavier than me—not fat necessarily, but not runway model thin either.

"How did the meeting go?" she asks, sipping a banana smoothie. She makes sure to have one everyday around lunchtime.

"It went well. They liked our work and want to see proposed media plans for Los Angeles, New York, and Dallas. I'm working on that now."

"Okay, well keep me posted, we really need to win this account."

"Definitely, I sure will." Ann is demanding sometimes and very persistent. Our office has the highest revenue for the region year after year, and she wants to keep it that way. I don't mind because that means job security for me.

I'm a popular woman today. Soon as Ann leaves, Mrs. Feinstein comes in. "Hello sweetie, how are you today?"

"I'm doing great! How about yourself?"

"Hey, it's Friday, I can't complain. I just wish I were glowing like you are," she says, sitting down making herself at home.

"Glowing? What are you talking about?"

"Well, you seem like your normal self again. Did you and Greg patch things up?"

"Actually, we decided to slow things down a bit, you know, spend some time apart."

She curiously glances at my bare ring finger. "Oh!" Her sleepy eyes widen, "Well, why are you so bubbly—this week's not even pay week?"

"Well, I—"

Mrs. Feinstein holds up both hands and stops me. "Wait a minute...you've met some super stud hunk, eh, eh?"

"Mrs. Feinstein!" I laugh.

"C'mon sweetie, I was your age thir—not too long ago, I know that look! What's his name?"

Mrs. Feinstein is making me feel like a preteen girl with a secret. "His name is Leron. But we're just friends—I've known him less than two weeks."

"Leron, eh? That sounds so...powerful and masculine. So, is he a stud or what? With a name like that, he has to be. Is he? Is he?"

I'm trying to keep from smiling, but I can't. "Yes, he's a ...stud," I giggle. I've never used the word 'stud' to describe a man but it seems to fit, what the heck!

"Look at you, smiling from ear to ear. How does his grandfat— never mind that, how does his father look?" she bats her eyes, stroking her hair.

Jokingly with a hand over my mouth I say, "Mrs. Feinstein, you're a married woman!"

"Hey sweetie, I just want to look at the merchandise, I don't have to touch it!" I can't help laughing again. I'm not sure what she's taking, but I need some of it too! "Just remember hon', take things slowly—you're still engaged, you know."

Ann peeks in again. "Harriet, did you make those copies yet?"

"I'll have them to you in five minutes."

"Very good," Ann says, disappearing down the hallway.

Mrs. Feinstein rolls her eyes. "I can't stand that woman! Gotta go, sweetie. Harriet, did you make those copies yet, blah, blah, blah," she whines, mocking Ann. "Do you *think* I made the copies? If I *did* make the stupid copies, you'd have them already," she mumbles walking out of the door. Mrs. Feinstein has a lot of fire for an older woman!

I finish reading the joke she sent, and then start working on those media plans for an hour nonstop. In the middle of spellchecking, she buzzes me.

"Greg's on line three."

I shake my head in disbelief. "Tell him I'm in a meeting, please." I don't feel like talking—I want to stay in a good mood. And why is he calling me at work anyway?

Thirty minutes later, my girl Tonya stops in. She's petite but loud—sometimes her voice sounds like fingernails scraping a chalkboard. She loves money and currently dates some second-string wide receiver from the Atlanta Falcons.

"Knock, knock. Hey girl, what you doin' for lunch?"

I glance up from the computer screen. "I'll probably just eat at my desk. I need to finish these media plans—"

"Eat at your desk? Girl c'mon, let's go to lunch—it's Friday! I'm buying."

"In that case, I know a real expensive steakhouse on Peachtree!"

"Don't try me this day," she laughs. "I'm comin' to get you in ten minutes—be ready!"

"Okay, mother," I reply as she twists out the office. *That girl is too grown for me*, I laugh to myself.

▼

We decide to eat at *Chin Chin's* Chinese restaurant on Roswell Road where many people from our office complex eat lunch. From top executives to janitors, everyone enjoys the inexpensive yet delicious food. Tonya and I decide to eat outside on the wooden patio deck since it's a pleasant day with a nice breeze blowing. Halfway into our meal she suspiciously glances over her shoulder before telling me what happened to her last night. The people around us are laughing, joking, and enjoying the nice weather, uninterested in her story but she doesn't begin talking until she is certain no one besides me is 'hearing her business.' She goes through the usual story of how her man isn't any good and how she should let him go. I've heard it so many times I almost have it memorized.

"Girl, me and David had a fight last night." *He ain't no good, girl,* I recite in my head. "He ain't no good, girl," she says as expected.

"What are you two fighting about now?"

"He got mad 'cause I said I didn't trust him."

"Well, do you?"

"No, unh uh. I know he messin' around, all these gold diggin' women just throwin' themselves at him just because he's in the NFL." She sounds hypocritical seeing how she did the exact same thing. And she has no room to complain about David fooling around when she's fooled around too—with several of his married teammates to be exact. "He swore up and down he wasn't cheatin'. He said I could call any number on his cell phone if I didn't believe him."

"Either he's really, really faithful or really stupid!" I open a bottle of soy sauce and ask, "Did you?"

"No, girl. He says I don't love him like he loves me. He says we can't build a healthy relationship not trusting each other," she stirs her sweet ice tea. "He made me feel real guilty. But everything is fine now. We made up." Now she is about to tell me about how good he is in bed—same old, same old—different day, same story. "...And when I say made up, I mean *made* up."

Yeah, yeah, we made love all night long, I repeat in my head before she can say it.

"We made love all night long!" she says.

He's like an engine, I continue reciting quietly to myself.

"He's like an engine, girl—all that conditionin' from football. But I told him he better wash his thang before touchin' me—you know he not circumcised. I ain't tryin' to catch no infections."

Suddenly my shrimp fried rice doesn't taste so good. "Don't mind me, I'm not trying to eat, *Tonya!*"

She quickly apologizes. "Sorry. So, how come you ain't tell me about your new man?"

"New man?"

"Yeah, Leon, Leray, whatever his name." My goodness. Rumors get around the office like the flu. Wait until I see Mrs. Feinstein.

I pause in the middle of cutting my egg roll and answer, "Because he's not my *man*. Greg is my *man*, okay?"

"Whatever, who is he then?"

"Just a friend. He installed my alarm system, we had coffee, and that was that."

"You like him, I see it all over you," she says suspiciously with a mouth full of beef teriyaki.

"He's just an alarm guy. Why would I waste my time with an *alarm guy* when I'm engaged to a fine, successful, intelligent *Senior Software Engineer*?" Tonya squints her eyes, shakes her head. She doesn't believe me. I'm trying to conceal my feelings, but she knows me too well.

"Girl, get real. Greg is a workaholic, and you love attention—that just doesn't mix—you hear what I'm sayin'?" I cut my egg roll into a thousand pieces—I don't know what else to do with my hands. "And why did you go giving him that ring back? That was a ROCK! I told you to never give back jewelry, why don't you ever listen to me?"

"I didn't feel right wearing it."

Tonya almost falls backwards in the chair. "WHAT?"

"Tee, I really like Leron. He's so attentive. He listens to every word I say like it's the last time he'll ever hear my voice. He's sweet and considerate—but I'm engaged to Greg and...and...I don't know."

"I'm gonna tell you like this." Tonya points her fork at me, moving it with every word, "You called off the engagement once you handed Greg that ring but I don't think you should be jumpin' in another relationship—Leron probably just another SP anyway."

"Another what?"

"SP. Self-proclaimed player." Tonya takes another bite of food, "You know, men who gotta line for everything and swear they're God's gift to women."

"Well, I'm trying to take things as slow as possible, but my feelings are growing so strong, so fast."

11

"...You have a good point. I'm trying to take things as slow as possible, but my feelings are growing so strong, so fast," I explain to Femia. I'm sitting shirtless on the edge of the bed, playing with the mesh lining of my basketball shorts. It's 6:50 p.m. and my screensaver has been flashing *Leron's Computer* for the last fifteen minutes.

"You sure you're not just horny?"

"If that were the case, I woulda called one of them chicken-heads. But I wanted a meaningful conversation—so I called you."

"Gosh, I've never heard you talk about a woman like this, she's really made an impression on you."

"She has. I mean, she's not shallow and materialistic like most of these chicks; she doesn't look down on me 'cause I'm not a white-collar business suit type. She's independent, passionate about life and her career, and she looks dynamite in a short skirt and heels."

"Boy, do you ever quit?"

"I'm just telling you the truth. You've known me since I was a lil' peewee, I'ma man now!"

"I thought you said she was engaged? That's bugging me."

I respond by telling her that Michelle wasn't wearing her engagement ring last night. Femia says it doesn't matter 'cause she's still involved with someone.

"Yeah but they're on the rocks," I reply. I know she's probably twisting the phone cord by now, pretending it's my neck.

"That makes it even worse," she says. "She's just in need of some time and attention—you just happen to be the one giving it. Once she's satisfied, who's to say she doesn't run back to him?"

"Well maybe—"

"Leron, I just don't want to see you get hurt. Just be careful, okay? I have to go study, my first midterm is Monday."

After me and Femia hang up, I reflect on our conversation for a few minutes, then get back to writing. Ra'ed calls shortly afterwards to see if I wanna go with him and Dave to the Gentlemen's Lair later on tonight. I tell him maybe some other time. I think I just better stay home and work on my book—especially after what happened last Friday night.

Even though, the clock says it's only 7:46 p.m., my eyelids feel five pounds heavy. Concentrating becomes impossible. I begin typing words twice—I need a break. After throwing two frozen entrees in the microwave, I plop on the sofa; one leg hangs off the side, the other across the arm; both hands are folded on my stomach. Like a stone sitting on the bottom of a pond, I lay motionless. Eventually, the low whisper of the television lulls me to sleep. Soon I'm in another dream as strange as the others.

I'm driving down a busy street when a state trooper appears in my rear view mirror. I'm not speeding and haven't broken any laws. Steadily he drives, weaving in and outta cars, tailing me close. Gradually as cars turn off to other destinations, me and him are still on the road—he still hasn't pulled me over—he only follows. I change lanes. He changes lanes. I turn left. He turns left. He continues to follow, never signaling me to pull over. Annoyed by the blatant harassment, I pull over anyway.

We're off to the side of the road where he sits behind me waiting like a bullfrog eyeing a fly. It takes at least ten minutes before he even opens the patrol car door. I gather my papers from the glove compartment—I know the routine well.

A female trooper walks to the window.

"Get out of the car."

"What's going on, what did I do wrong? Here's my license and registra—"

"Get out of the car, now!"

I unfasten my seatbelt and get out.

She takes off her cap and shades, looking at me with a crooked, devious smile. It's Anesia! My entire central nervous system freezes. A hard knot tightens in my throat preventing me from speaking. She laughs harder, while I struggle to form words.

"You're a dog, so I'm going to treat you like one." She blows the whistle around her neck and suddenly two German Shepherds jump outta the car. One bites my leg while the other launches at my chest, knocking me to the ground. I'm pleading for her to call them off. She responds with another menacing laugh.

I cover my head as the dogs shake me from side-to-side, growling and panting. When I manage to stagger to my feet, the weight of their heavy bodies pin me back down. Their sharp incisors rip through my jeans. Hot saliva oozes from their jaws onto my legs. Their breath gets hotter with each bone-crushing bite. Easily they tear through my skin, revealing my bloody inner flesh. I cry out. Anesia stands emotionless, arms folded, enjoying my suffering—.

Immediately my eyes open. I haven't had a nightmare since I was a kid. This one seemed so real; I wiggle my legs to make sure it wasn't. I look at the clock again: 9:19 p.m. It feels much later. A lasagna smell in the air reminds me of the frozen dinners I left in the microwave. After reheating my delicious bachelor cuisine, I sit down to enjoy, overlooking the fact it's bland, 'cause it's quick and easy to fix. Plus, the only meal I can cook is spaghetti.

I'm not surprised when the phone rings. People usually call me while I'm eating, sleeping or using the bathroom. I dunno why it happens like this—but it does—it's all good, though.

"Hey Leron, it's me, Michelle. Did I catch you in the middle of eating?"

"Hey you," I say, mouth stuffed with sweet corn. "Oh, I was just finishing."

"You cook?"

"Ah... yeah, all the time. I love to cook." Okay, maybe I don't but I know women love a man that cooks. Besides, I do cook—spaghetti!

"My, my, a man who cooks—women love that."

"Really?" I ask, as if learning something new.

"Yes, I think it's sexy. So, why aren't you out on this beautiful

Friday night, Leron?"

"I'm kinda tired, I'ma hang out at home tonight. What are you getting into?"

"Actually, my girl and I just got back from a movie. She went to her boyfriend's house and left me here bored."

"Where's Greg?" I slam a palm against my forehead when I realize what I said. I probably shouldn't have asked that but it's too late now.

Pretending not to hear me, she says, "I have something I want to show you."

"You got something to show me, huh?" I repeat—smooth and mellow, of course.

"Yes, yes I do." Her voice has a knee-weakening sugar-coated warmth.

"What is it?"

"Not going to tell."

"Gimme a clue."

"Okay, you can ask two yes or no questions, that's it."

I pause a second and ask, "Is it something I can...feel?" I ain't beating around the bush.

"Yes, you can feel it..."

"Ummm...will I enjoy it?" I ask. I can't tell if she's toying with me or not.

"That depends, but I think you will."

"Well, when you gonna show me, girl? You got my mind wonderin' now."

"When do you want me to?" she asks. Her voice sounds as anxious as mine.

"I ain't doing anything, what about tonight?" I say half-joking, half-serious.

"Okay."

I hesitate until her response registers in my brain. "Are you serious?"

"Yes, you're not?"

"Oh, uh, yeah, yeah, let me give you directions."

Michelle doesn't seem like the super freaky type but those are the ones you gotta watch out for. I'm not complaining. I just gotta clean this place up some. Where's that stupid dustpan? I still need to shower. I gotta change my linen. Where's my slow jam CD? I still haven't cleaned the bathroom. I've been so busy writing that I've neglected simple household things. I haven't cleaned my crib since Tierra came over and that was a month ago!

I've been cleaning like crazy ever since I got off the phone. Now It's 10:21 p.m. and Michelle gonna be here any minute. Everything is straight except my bedroom. It looks like those tornadoes from the *Wizard of Oz* came through; clean clothes are scattered on the bed, dirty ones on the floor, shoes and socks are everywhere. Time is dwindling. I throw the clean clothes in the dresser and everything else under the bed—she'll never see under there anyway.

I think I heard Michelle knocking at the door but I'm not sure. I answer right before she's getting back into her car.

"Leaving me already?"

She turns around, putting her keys away. She's wearing black jeans and a burgundy blouse. I'm trying to see every curve I can. "I didn't think anybody was home."

"Sorry about that, come in, come in." As she strolls inside, I watch her from behind, salivating over her custom-made frame, built just for me. She looks around my place as if checking for termites. "Sorry it's so plain, been too busy to really decorate."

"It's fine, nice and cozy."

"Yeah, but it's missing something elegant and sophisticated—so why don't you go sit in the living room," I smile. "Can I get you anything to drink?"

Sitting on the sofa like a sweet princess on a throne she answers, "I'm fine, maybe later."

"How was the movie?" I ask, taking my rightful spot on the throne next to her.

"It was okay, I guess. We went to Lenox Square. It was so ghetto. People kept yelling and cursing at the screen...and laughing at scenes that weren't even supposed to be funny. I couldn't really enjoy it."

I nod. This is funny. I find her petty frustration cute. "It's Friday night, you gotta go earlier to avoid the hood rats. I thought everybody knew that."

"Well, I haven't gone to the movies in a while, I don't know."

"You might wanna try a matinee next time," I laugh and then ask how her day went. She tells me about the contracts she negotiated, a potential new client she met today, and her uptight boss who's been getting on her nerves.

"Enough about me, how was your day?" she asks.

"Well, I gotta really bad paper cut filling out some forms," I joke, holding up my thumb for inspection.

"You're so crazy, you make me laugh!" She reaches in her purse.

The size of it reminds me of my backpack in middle school. But I know how women are. They have a purse for every type of occasion. She pulls outta folded piece of paper and hands it to me.

"What's this?"

"Well, read it and see."

I unfold it and scan the contents:

The Stronger Me

By: Michelle Barkley

"Oh, you wrote a poem?" I ask, glancing at the page, then her.

"You inspired me to write again. I wrote this earlier. I'm rusty, so it's not very good." Her irresistible innocent eyes connect with mine.

I hand the poem back. "Read it to me."

Staring at me like a stranger offering her candy, she hesitates and says, "No, it's stupid. You won't even like it."

"Go on, read it to me." She runs her fingers through her hair and reads:

"Deep down in my mortal soul, is another me waiting to unfold.

Another me daring and bold, another me grasping for dreams to hold..."

Her voice crackles in the beginning. As she continues, it grows distinctive and pronounced. I look. I listen. I stare; I admire, mesmerized by her sincerity. I study her lips. My roaming eyes wander to her soft, trembling hands loosely clutching the page.

"...The weaker me has given way, to a stronger me seizing today.

Discovering where ambitions lay, rising above what others say.

The stronger me has come to fore, higher in the sky I soar.

Knocking down every closed door, the stronger me I now adore."

She folds the paper in half, returning it to the handbag. "Okay, what do you think?" she asks, squinting her eyes. I guess she thinks I'ma rip the poem apart or something.

"I think—"

She cuts me off before I can finish. "Please don't lie. You promise to tell the truth?"

"I promise."

"Okay," she says, relaxed and satisfied.

"I liked it. It was deep and passionate. I know you put a lot of effort into it. I'm glad you started writing again," I smile. "...And listening to your words and watching you say them captivated me."

"Oh stop! You're just trying to make me not feel bad!"

I slide closer to her. "No, seriously. That's why I wanted you to read it. I wanted to hear *your* voice and *your* words. How did you feel reading it?"

"I'm not sure," she plays with her fingers. "At first...at first I was nervous, but as I kept reading, I felt better. I felt more confident. I've never read my poetry to anyone!"

"Really? I didn't mean to make you feel awkward."

She strokes my arm. "No, actually...I felt very comfortable with you." When our eyes meet, we lean closer, and lightly kiss. She pulls away to look into my eyes again. "I feel so light right now," she giggles, patting her chest.

"That's a *good* thing."

"Well, I'm glad you liked it. I couldn't wait to show it to you."

We talk a lil' more but I wanna take the party to the bedroom. She wants to watch movies. I act like I wanna watch movies too. I'm still trying to take it easy with her. I don't wanna make any wrong moves and mess anything up.

By the end of the second DVD, we're zombies. Delirious, I nod in and out occasionally glancing at the black and white static on television. Michelle is leaning on my shoulder—knocked out—she lost the fight an hour ago. My arm is around her to keep her from falling over. I can't believe it's 2:33 a.m. Time has flown.

"Michelle," I whisper. "Michelle." I lightly shake her shoulder.

Her eyes partially open, she finally responds. "...Huh? What time is it?" she moans, snuggling closer in my arm.

"Two-thirty."

"I better...get...g-going," she yawns.

"No, I'm not letting you get on the road half asleep. You can have my bed, okay?" She dozes off again. "Michelle? C'mon let's go, you can sleep in my bed." I manage to get her on her feet. Her limp body leans back against mine.

"W-Where's my purse...and...my keys...?"

"They're fine. C'mon," I hold her as we stumble down the hallway to my bedroom. I pull the sheets back before she drops on the bed. "Okay, gimme your foot, let's take these shoes off." I look at her and laugh. She's sitting straight up with her eyes closed. "There, now gimme the other one."

"...I shouldn't stay, I need to g—"

"You ain't getting on the road this late, I told you. Now lay down." Scratching her head, smacking her lips, she collapses on the pillow and doesn't say another word. I cover her, grab the other pillow, and stagger out to the couch.

I can't fall asleep. All I can think about is how angelic Michelle looks curled up in my bed. I wish I were curled up beside her. Of course, making love crosses my mind more than once but I woulda been just as happy holding her until morning. There must be something special about her 'cause I ain't never felt like this.

12

I wake up to a faint scent of Leron's cologne and the Saturday morning sun creeping through the blinds, shining across my face. On the pillow next to me is a cute stuffed puppy; to the right is an alabaster statue of Shakespeare. As I yawn and stretch, the sheets slide off my chest, down to my waist. I glance at the clock on the nightstand. 8:48 a.m. I take a deep breath, running a hand through my hair—it's a mess! I wish I could've wrapped it before falling asleep. I take a red scrunchy from my purse and pull my hair into a ponytail. I slip on my shoes, grab my keys sitting next to the lamp, and go look for Leron. It's been a long time since I've slept in any man's bed other than Greg's and it feels somewhat awkward.

The lights and television are both on. With one shoe off and one on, Leron is stretched across the sofa snoring loudly, arms folded across his chest. He finally wakes up after I shake him a few times.

"I'm leaving," I whisper.

"Uh...wait." He scratches the side of his face, "You wanna get some breakfast or something?"

I kiss his cheek and smile. "No, I'm fine, finish sleeping."

He jumps to his feet, walks me to my car, and doesn't return inside until I drive around the corner. I check my cell phone messages as I'm leaving the apartment complex.

First message recorded yesterday, 9:42 p.m.: "Girl, me and David had another fight. I need to talk to you, call me soon as you get in—"

Second message recorded yesterday, 10:31 p.m.: "Michelle, where you at? Call me—"

Third message recorded yesterday 11:57 p.m.: "Girl it's 12:00 a.m., you ain't home and your cell phone's off—what are you doing?—"

Fourth message recorded today, 12:29 a.m.: "MICHELLE? Bye—!"

Four new voicemail messages and all of them are from Tonya. She can be annoying at times, but at least she cares about my welfare. I better call and let her know everything is fine.

"Hey, Tee, it's me—"

"GIRL! Where have you been? I called you four or five times last night. Me and David had another fight. I needed to talk to you."

"I went to Leron's to watch some movies."

"Leron's, huh?"

"Yeah, I fell asleep and ended up staying over. It was late."

"Staying over, huh?"

I hate when she repeats what I say, it's annoying. "Nothing happened, so don't even go there; I slept in his bed, he slept on the sofa. He took my shoes off for me and even tucked me in. He was a perfect gentleman."

"Lemme get this straight. You stayed at a man's house, IN HIS BED, late at night—and he didn't try a thing?"

"I'm not going to answer you anymore, girl. I told you nothing happened."

"I don't like this, Michelle. Y'all spending a lot of time together, and you still stringing Greg along."

"I'm not stringing anybody along. I told him I needed time, and I do."

"Time to run around with some alarm guy?"

"We don't run, we drive!"

"Don't play wit' me, Chelle."

"Well, I have fun with Leron."

"Uh huh. Having fun might get you hurt. I don't wanna say I told you so."

"Good, don't."

I know Tonya is trying to look out for me, but sometimes she can be pushy. Her close-mindedness doesn't help much either. Even still, I always listen to her advice—I just rarely follow it. My mother always said never take advice from anyone who isn't doing better than you.

Tonya's motto about men and relationships is: the way to a man's heart is through his bedroom, not his stomach—and she lives by it! All she and David do is fight, have sex, then fight again afterwards. She knows he's unfaithful. Deep down inside I don't think she cares. She just wants to feel loved and wanted. Maybe him banging her brains out in a million sexual maneuvers gives her those feelings. Who knows?

To get her off my back about Leron, I ask about David. She sighs and says the Falcons are trading him to the San Francisco Forty-Niners. He leaves in a week and says he'll send for her once he gets situated. What she really wants is for him to propose but every time she brings up marriage, he changes the subject.

"I don't think he wanna marry me and I don't wanna waste my time. That's what our fight was about last night," she says. "If he actually moves me out there, things might work. And if it doesn't, his friend Gerald is waiting to take his place. He plays tight end, and his end is sho' nuff tight, if you know what I mean!"

"Girl, you're a hot mess!"

"I'm just joking. But I gotta go, he's in the room and I don't wanna keep him waitin' long, know what I'm sayin'? See ya!"

I ease up the driveway into my garage by the time our conversation ends. A few hours later, I decide to do some house cleaning. I turn on the radio and pull back the beige cloth curtains in the living room to let the sun shine through. I put on an old sweat suit and some rubber gloves to protect my hands from the bleach and Pine Sol I use to clean the kitchen. The phone rings as I'm getting the mop from the closet. It's Greg. After we exchange our habitual hellos, he asks how I'm doing. To be nice, I ask him the same.

"I'm surviving," he says. "I called you at work yesterday but I didn't leave a message—you know I hate voicemails— they're too impersonal. I miss you, baby."

"Greg, it hasn't even been that long."

"My point exactly. And if I'm miserable after such a short while, imagine me if this keeps up."

"Well, I'm sorry but—"

"Have you had enough time yet? I can't take this much longer."

"Greg, I can't lie, I think about you sometimes, but I've felt like a new woman lately; I'm getting out more, writing poetry again, work is good..."

"Well, guess what," his voice hints of excitement. "The project is done. Finished. No more stressful nights."

"That's wonderful. You worked hard, you deserve a break."

"The vice-president was very impressed, so impressed that he promoted me. Now I have less work and more time...more time to spend with you, baby. Isn't that great?"

"That's fine I guess, but what happens when the next big project rolls around? We'll be back at square one again."

"Oh, no! I'm not letting this happen again. Over the past few weeks I've had a chance to experience life without you—I can't stand it..." He pauses as if trying to figure out the best way to say his next sentence. "...Why don't you come over tonight? We can have a romantic night out on the town. How about it?"

"I can't, I have things to do."

"Look, I understand. Take all day to think about it. Call me later on and let me know what time to pick you up."

"Greg, I don't need to think a—"

"I love you baby, bye, bye," he says, hurrying off the line. Rolling my eyes at the phone, I shake my head and hang up. Am I doing the right thing? The more time I spend with Leron, the further my feelings for Greg suppress. I know Leron is a bit of a ladies' man, but he seems sincere and genuine with me. Maybe he sees something the others failed to see. During the last few months, I've built walls around myself, but he's broken through them. He's brought out the best in me in such a short time. My self-esteem is higher. I'm surer of myself and much bolder than I've ever been. He makes me feel like I'm the most important thing in his world.

13

I did it. I persuaded Michelle to let me take her to dinner. She's really feeling me now, especially after spending the night last weekend. I call to let her know I'm on the way. Me and Femia talk for a minute right after that. Today I bought my plane ticket to go see her graduate. Normally I wait until the last minute for these kinda things, but I wanna make sure nothing goes wrong. This means a lot to her, she's worked real hard and I wanna see her walk. It seems like she's been in school forever. She's one of the few people I know who actually loves school, always studying, always learning—a real bookworm. I know for a fact she'll be the first to read my book when I finish. She says midterms didn't go as well as she would've liked— which probably means she got all A's and one B instead of straight A's. After telling me about exams, she mentions she's taking a job in Dallas. A financial consulting firm gave her a good offer and they'll pay for school if she wants to get an MBA. All she has to do is graduate. I thought the last year of college was supposed to be a breeze, but the same day midterms were over, she started getting ready for final exams! The conversation ends with her rushing off to a study group.

I pull into Michelle's driveway and stop to think before getting out. It's been over two months since we bumped into each other in the lobby. We've been spending more time together and now we're calling each other pet names like: baby, sugar, and honey. But I told her not to call me "boo." I can't stand being called "boo" 'cause it reminds me of that psycho chick.

I get outta my ride chuckling to myself at the thought of introducing Michelle to Spurt. I know I must be serious about her to introduce her to him! Well, she gotta get used to him sooner or later. I called him earlier this week to holler since I haven't seen him in a while. He said he's been busy working, spending time with his son, and kicking it with the new chick he met at the shop. He carried on about the girl like she's flawless, talking about how smart and classy she is. I never heard him brag about how *smart* a girl is. He told me they've gone to poetry readings, book signings, and even the museum! Spurt went to a museum! I gotta see this chick! Maybe he needs a woman like that to tone him down some. He's bringing her tonight so he made sure to remind me about our bet. Yeah, I lost. I'll hit him up with the hundred dollars at dinner.

▼

Inside the restaurant, big band jazz streams outta the wall-mounted speakers. The atmosphere is loud and it seems like every five minutes I hear that stupid happy birthday routine. No seats are available when me and Michelle arrive. I dunno why I didn't make reservations—it's the weekend, I knew the wait would be long. Fortunately, we only waited ten or fifteen minutes before getting seated at a corner booth in nonsmoking. We're sitting close, chatting, laughing, and waiting for Spurt and his girl.

"So, is Spurt the one that's in Romeo and Juliet?" Michelle asks. During the drive here, I asked if she wanted to go with me to see Ra'ed in Romeo and Juliet next week. I laugh when a picture of Spurt playing Romeo appears in my head.

"No, that's Ra'ed. Spurt is the one I've known since third grade. I wanted to meet his new girlfriend, and he wanted to meet you. We decided to do it over dinner."

"Well, I hope I don't make you look bad."

"Don't worry about that. You make me look good just by sitting here!"

"Oh, quit it!" She slaps my shoulder and smiles.

"I almost forgot, I should tell you that uh... well, Spurt is a little *rough* around the edges, but he means well."

Michelle raises an eyebrow. "What do you mean *rough?*"

"You'll see. Oh, and don't shake his hand."

"Uh... okay?" Looking past my face, her eyes suddenly enlarge. "Ann?" Spurt and his new girl arrive. I turn around to greet them and see Spurt and...and ANESIA! She's the girl he's been bragging about all this time, the psycho chick? I try lifting my heavy lower lip—it refuses. Looking at Spurt, then Anesia, Michelle, then back at Anesia, my eyeballs bounce around in their sockets. I feel like someone just drilled a tiny hole in the top of my head and snatched my stomach through it.

"Michelle? What a surprise!" Anesia says, cutting her eyes at me.

"You two already know each other?" Spurt says, waiting for Anesia to sit.

"We work together, boo."

"Yeah, Ann's my supervisor." All of a sudden, I feel queasy. I wish somebody would hit me with a spiked bat and put me outta my misery.

"Small world, huh?" Spurt says. *Way too small,* I think to myself. I'll give him his hundred dollars plus another hundred to take Anesia back home! I manage to regain my senses long enough to introduce Spurt and Michelle.

"Spurt this is Michelle, Michelle, this is my man Spurt."

"Hello, Spurt."

He holds out is hand. Michelle glances at me then reluctantly shakes it. "How you doin'? Call me James, I don't go by Spurt no more." He looks at Anesia, "Nessie, says it sounds ghetto. Lee, this my baby, Ann. Ann, this my boy, Leron."

I slowly hold out my hand. I can't even fake a smile right now. "Hello," I mutter.

Her grip is firm and vise-like. "It's a pleasure to meet you," she says with a crooked smirk.

Spurt puts his arm around her, kissing her cheek. "This a good woman right here, man." I just nod. This is too crazy. Big as Atlanta is, how is this possible? "Sorry we late, Nessie made me change my clothes."

"Sure did. I told him he wasn't going anywhere with me dressed like a clown."

"Oh, really?" I reply. Spurt reads the 'you've turned into a punk' look on my face.

"Man, she looks after me—takes care of me." He sounds like a brainwashed idiot. My worst fears are confirmed—he's definitely whipped.

Anesia cuts her eyes at me again. "That's right, I know how to please my baby." She pinches his cheek, shaking it lightly.

"How did you two meet?" Michelle asks.

Anesia nudges Spurt's arm. "Tell her, boo."

"Well, I'm an Automotive Technician at a car repair shop, right..." As he's speaking, I ball my fist up beneath the table. Did he just say *Automotive Technician?* Earlier this week he was just a *'Mechanic.'*

"...And while I was checkin' her car out, I was checkin' *her* out too! I *had* to introduce myself," he says with a Velveeta cheese grin.

"...And I'm a sucker for a strong man in a uniform," Anesia adds, "How did you meet Leron, Michelle?"

"Well, I accidentally bumped into him in the lobby at work—I didn't think anything of it. A few days later, I called to have a security system installed. When I answered the door, to my surprise it was Leron." She looks at me and smiles, "I ended up getting a good security system *and* a good friend."

Anesia stares with an ice-cold look. "Isn't that nice..."

"Where the waiter at, I'm starvin'?" Spurt blurts out.

It takes nearly twenty-five minutes to get our food. Like a Kirby vacuum cleaner, I suck up my steak and baked potato. I'm doing all I can to make the night go faster. A brutal headache is throbbing in my head, my knotting stomach feels nasty and hot inside, and looking across the table at Anesia ain't helping. I actually thought I got rid of her, and now by some twisted coincidence, she's dating my best friend—has him sounding like a straight wuss! And on top of that, she's Michelle's boss? This is the kinda thing people watch on television. The nightmare I had, doesn't even compare to this—at least when I woke up, it ended. Now, I'm living one—an ugly one!

Anesia keeps cutting her eyes at me all night. I try to ignore her but I can't. Imagine the uneasiness of the whole thing. Picture everyone you know seeing you take a nice, long dump, and watching you wipe afterwards. Embarrassing. I know that's real nasty. But multiply that feeling by a hundred and that's a good idea of how I feel.

With an empty plate and a quarter-full glass, I'm ready to dip. Everyone is laughing and joking, they're all having such a lovely time. It seems like Anesia would've been somewhat reserved and uneasy too, but she's thriving in the moment. Rubbing and kissing Spurt all night; sharing office jokes with Michelle; glancing at me—she's eating this up.

"Why are you so quiet Leron?" she asks.

Michelle places her hand on my shoulder." Yeah, honey, you haven't said much tonight."

"I don't feel so good that's all." I scratch an imaginary itch on my forehead, "I think I'm coming down with something."

Spurt shakes his head, turns to Anesia and says, "If Lee's quiet for a long time, you know *something* gotta be wrong. I should know. We been down since the third grade."

"The third grade, boo?"

"Yup, the third grade."

"Well, tell us how you guys became friends, boo," Anesia says, knowing I don't feel like hearing this. She's doing her best to make the night longer than it needs to be and she's succeeding.

Completely clueless, Michelle plays along. "Yeah, I want to hear this!"

Spurt takes a quick taste of pink lemonade, smacks his lips, and begins the story. "...I remember when the teacher introduced him to the class. He had on an ugly pullover vest with a white long-sleeve shirt buttoned up all the way up to his neck. I'm telling you, he was goofy..."

"Aw, I bet you were a little cutie." Anesia interrupts, making this nasty looking goo-goo face at me.

"Still is." Michelle adds. I stare at both of them like knuckleheads, muting Spurt's—James'—*whatever*, voice outta my mind.

"What happened then, boo?"

With a mouth full of macaroni and cheese, Spurt continues to rattle. "...Um, oh, one day at recess I came up to him. He looked at me like I had a big wet booger on my face."

Anesia slaps Spurt's hand. "Boo, not at the dinner table!"

"Sorry, baby. I asked him how old he was and told him I was 'bout to be nine on October eighteenth—"

"Getting ready to turn nine," Anesia corrects him.

He scratches his head and says, "*Getting ready to turn* nine I mean." He looks at Anesia for approval. She smiles.

This is ridiculous. Maybe I should be telling some stories. Like how in ninth grade this chick he wanted liked me more than him. Out of jealousy he lied to the girl's older brother, told him I said something about his mama. I almost got beat down over that. I see he never tells those stories!

"James, they don't wanna hear any more of this dumb story, man," I grumble.

"Well, I want to hear it," Michelle says. "I think it's cute."

"Me too James, keep going, boo."

He gladly obliges babbling a good fifteen minutes while Anesia corrects his speech every other sentence. Is this the same dude that told me he ain't bending over backwards to please a girl 'cause they'll drive you crazy? He's definitely singing another tune now and I gotta interrupt it.

"...And everybody lived happily ever after. Waiter! We need our check. Y'all I'm ready to leave. My head is killing me."

"It's still early, dawg. We should all go see a movie," Spurt says.

"That' sounds like fun, boo."

I can't take another minute of this! I push my empty plate aside. "I'm not up for it tonight, y'all."

"Baby, you got some aspirin?" Spurt asks Anesia. "Let Lee have some, he'll be okay."

Anesia pulls out two gel tablets from her purse and slides them across the table. "These might help, Leron," she says, faking like she cares.

I look at her like she has two big zits on her face—actually, she does. "I'm cool, I just need to go home and get some sleep. Thanks, though."

Spurt doesn't wanna hear it, he keeps bugging me. "Ah c'mon man! We ain't hung out in a while. Take the pills, dawg," he insists, voraciously crunching on an ice cube. For the first time, I realize it's not *only* with women—Spurt doesn't understand the meaning of "no" from *anybody.*

I lean back from the table. "Man, Spurt, I'm—"

"James! Call me James from now on!"

"James, I told you I'm not feeling good." I give Michelle a desperate look and wait for her to take my side.

She rubs my hand. "Go ahead, honey, take them, you'll feel better." So much for taking my side, it's three against one. Outnumbered and outmatched, I take the stupid pills. Thirty minutes later, we go to the stupid theatre and watch a stupid movie.

▼

The phone rings the next morning while I'm knocked out recovering from last night. Rolling over to the nightstand, I answer.

"Poor baby, were you sleeping?" It's Anesia. What's her problem? "Are you still sick from last—"

"You had your fun, why you still buggin' me?"

"You're so grumpy wumpy when you're just waking up."

"What do you want?"

"So, Mr. Leron King. I see you're sleeping with my co-worker now; are you trying to make your way around the whole office? I can't stand men like you, going around playing with women's emotions. You just won't be satisfied will you?"

"You got me all wrong, chick."

"No, I think I have you all right! WHAT'S THAT LITTLE AIRHEAD HAVE THAT I DON'T? What makes her so special?"

I roll outta bed on to my feet, release a deep breath into the receiver and ask, "Are you done?"

"I'm just beginning, I got something for you and that whore—" She hangs up. Why someone would turn something so small into a huge personal vendetta is beyond me. She comes straight from lunatic city, population—her. I immediately call Michelle to make sure things are cool. She's fine and asks am I feeling better. I tell her I'm okay, just gonna relax and read the Sunday paper. She starts talking about the great time she had last night. But thinks it's weird Anesia is dating Spurt. She didn't think Anesia went for his type. She must not know that chick will probably go for *anyone,* long as they're breathing and walking upright. I'm just relieved she hasn't done anything crazy yet.

I sit the phone back in its cradle and put on my housecoat. While I'm outside getting the Sunday newspaper, somebody in a red BMW blows their horn twice. I almost jump outta my skin when Anesia pops outta the car in a pink robe, head full of green hair rollers. Her eyes are big and puffy, it looks like she just woke up.

"It's about time! I waited three hours for you to come outside," she yawns. I still don't believe what's happening. The whole time we were on the phone she was right outside my crib? Girl definitely not wrapped too tight. Maybe I should be a lil' scared 'cause this is some murderous, stalker-type stuff. I dunno what's going through this chick's head. She snaps her fingers and gets in her sister-girl stance. "...I want you to know I'm not one to mess with, Leron King!"

"Why are you so bitter? Just leave me alone. I was up front and honest with you—that wasn't enough. I tried to be your friend—that wasn't enough. What do you want from—?"

"What do I want from you? I WANT YOU TO SUFFER! I want you to hurt like I've been hurt—over and over again." She steps closer, "I want you to feel pain like I have..."

I wave the newspaper in her face. "What you need to do is stop sniffing paint thinner, it kills your brain cells."

"Aren't we funny? One thing I liked about you was your sense of humor. You could've had more of this, boo." She parts her robe, flashing her naked body. I jump back at the sight of her, at the sight of it... all of it. She closes the robe after realizing my disgust. "It's a pity I have to make your life so miserable, boo. Poor, poor James, and that adorable Michelle," she sighs. "It's a shame she has to suffer too. She's a bright girl—a slut, but bright nonetheless."

"If you do anything to Spurt or Mich—"

"Stop the weak macho routine. That's the problem with you men, always trying to control and manipulate. You have *no* power, and *no* control whatsoever," she snaps again, takes two steps towards her car, and turns back around. "What I want to know is...how does that make you feel, huh, Leron King? How does it feel being a man and not being in control?"

I march after her when she walks off and gets in the car. "You a psycho, you know that? A real psy—" Her revving engine drowns out my words. If my neighbors weren't already awake, they definitely are now and they're probably watching this craziness too.

"I'm done, you bore me," Anesia says, putting on a pair of shades.

"Besides, James is detailing my car later today. Speaking of cars, how's yours running...*SUGAR?*" she laughs, backing outta the parking space. Her words are beating inside me like an off-key xylophone. Too many congested thoughts swell in my head: She's the one who sabotaged my ride? Was she the one constantly calling my job without leaving any messages? What's she gonna do next? What'd she mean Michelle has to suffer? Why's she bringing Spurt into this? I honestly believe she'll do something else crazy and that makes me uneasy.

With all the strength I can muster this early in the morning, I throw the whole Sunday newspaper at her car. It hits the lower front windshield, bouncing off the hood with a loud thud. Anesia sticks her head outta the window to blow me a sarcastic kiss before flicking me off and speeding away.

▼

Sunday and Monday creep by. It's been torturous waking up each day wondering if anything crazy is gonna happen. But I gotta just get on with life. I know one thing, though, I've been staying home a lot more! I guess that's good 'cause I've been getting a lot of writing done. It's Tuesday evening and I'm glancing over my book; a few more chapters to go and the rough draft will be finished. It still needs a lot of work, but at least I have a foundation. I'm not sure if I'm more exhausted than excited or more excited than exhausted. I guess more excited 'cause I wanna sit here and keep writing. But my stomach has other ideas. Tonight I'm meeting all the guys at an all-you-can-eat buffet in midtown. X wants everyone together before he tells us "the news." The rest of the fellas know about the lay-off, but still don't know about the engagement. I do of course, but I'll act surprised.

We agree to meet at 6:30 p.m.—it's 7:10 p.m., and Spurt is late. We're trying to wait for him but he's taking forever. Ra'ed and Dave start eating salad; me and X just sip our drinks.

"Where's Spurt?" X says, a small wrinkle shifting on his forehead, "I want everybody to hear this at the same time."

"I haven't seen him since Saturday night," I tell him.

"Why don't you just tell us now?" Dave asks. "We'll fill him in when he gets here."

X sips his coke. "No, I'm only saying it once."

"I bet I know where he is. He's with his new girl," I huff. "She got him wrapped around her ugly lil' finger."

"Why did you say *ugly* little finger?"

"If you saw her, you'd know what I'm talking about."

X laughs. "Oh, okay. She's got the kind of face that would make an onion cry, huh?" We all laugh as Spurt trots to the table. "There he is," X shouts throwing up his hands.

"What up, what up, my Negroes, Indians, and White boys. My ears itchin' so y'all musta been talkin' 'bout me." He sits down and brags about Anesia giving him a massage after work. One thing led to another and he lost track of time.

Ra'ed shakes the ice in his drink and says, "Okay X, we're all here. What's up?"

X slides his drink to the side and makes eye contact with us. "I'm not going to beat around the bush, Lisa and I are engaged."

We all congratulate him. We all know it's about time they got engaged.

"Thanks fellas. Now which one of you guys is next?" We look around like he's speaking to somebody at another table.

"My mother already nags me, I don't need a wife doing the same," Dave says.

X looks down at the carpet, then back at us. "... I got some more news..."

This time I'm puzzled. I thought I knew all of X's "news." Now I'm curious. "Man, don't tell me Lisa's pregnant."

"Pregnant? No, I got a new job." He says he's had several offers but turned them all down. I don't blame him. He wanted to get as much loot as possible, especially since he's getting married. Shoot, he's gonna need it—the way Lisa spends money! That girl runs through cash like diarrhea through a newborn.

"Congrats again!"

"That didn't take you long," Spurt says.

"Nope, and I couldn't pass up this one. I'll be making more money, with less responsibility—and that means less stress. They're even going to pay my living expenses for my first three months and give me a company car too."

"True, you can't beat that, man!"

"...The only thing is." X plays with the straw in his root beer, "The only thing is they want me to move to Indiana..."

"Indiana?"

Dave wipes his mouth with a folded napkin and asks, "What's so hot about Indiana? There's nothing there but hillbillies and NASCAR."

"That's where the main office is."

"Why can't you just work here?" I ask.

"Actually I can, but it'll take me two years to reach the position they're offering me right now up there."

"So what are you gonna do?"

"I still don't know. It's a hard decision. My whole life is here, my family, my boys—everything. But then I have to think about Lisa and our future."

"We all want you to stay, man. But honestly, you should take the job up there. If it don't work out, you can always come back to Atlanta," I tell him.

Ra removes his elbows from the table. "But you don't know anyone there—no family, no friends."

X clears his throat and takes a deep breath. "I know...I'll just have to start from scratch."

The rest of dinner is kinda bittersweet. We're happy X is engaged, and that he has a new job, but the moving thing...man! After dinner, we hit a few bars down in Buckhead until about one o'clock. It slips my mind that I have to get up early tomorrow morning. I've been too busy trying to have a good time with X and the fellas. This might be one of last times we kick it.

▼

The next day after work, 'cause I had no problems or difficult customers, I decide it's gonna be a spaghetti night! I bounce to the store to get noodles and garlic bread. I already have some meat that's been in the freezer for a week.

The grocery store is crowded and the lines are long and slow. My line has a ninety-year-old bagboy and a cashier wearing glasses with four-inch thick lenses. I'm reading a magazine article about some lady giving birth to a wolf boy while I wait my turn. The cashier scans my food and then scratches his head when the computer beeps.

"The computer is having trouble reading the magnetic strip. I'll just type in the numbers, one second, please." I tap my fingers on the counter and wait. Again, he scratches his head. "Sir, I'm sorry, but this card was declined."

"Declined, what do you mean? This card is brand new, I haven't even used it yet." The cashier tightens his lips and stares with a stupid expression. "I'll just pay cash, how much is it again?"

"Five-sixty-two."

After opening my wallet, I realize I have no cash and the people behind me are getting restless; I feel all their eyes piercing my skin. "You guys gotta ATM?"

The cashier shakes his head. "No we don't, sorry. But there's one across the street." Frustrated, I start to walk off when an older woman offers to pay the total. Before I can say it's not necessary, she hands the cashier a ten-dollar bill and smiles at me, high cheekbones shining under the store lights. I smile back, but I've never been so embarrassed in my life. I thank her, and hurry outta the store to call the credit card company. I almost wanna slam my cell phone on ground when the customer service rep confirms it—my card *is* maxed out! Apparently, someone used my account information to buy an expensive surround sound system. Even though the rep tells me I have sixty days to dispute the purchase, I still feel violated. I've always been careful with my private information and now this?

14

When I arrived at 7:30, most of the lights were off. It's Wednesday morning and I'm one of the only people in this chilly office. Ann called me late last night in a panic saying she needs our client's media plans by 9:00 this morning. Frantically typing away, I try to complete in a few hours what normally takes a week; luckily, I manage to finish with a couple of minutes to spare. At 8:47, I printed the plans and made copies. Now it's 9:00 sharp and Ann has just walked into my office.

"Good morning, Michelle."

"Good morning. I just have to stack this last pile and everything will be ready to go."

"Oh, that's fantastic but I don't need them now."

I drop the papers on the desk. "Excuse me?"

"I don't need them now" She places her hands on her hips, "I asked the client for an extension. I guess I should've told you earlier but I was tied up on a phone call. Sorry about that."

"Okay, no problem," I smile when in actuality I want to rip Ann's head off! I've been rushing to get these plans done and she knew the whole time we had an extension?

"Thanks for your willingness to go the extra mile, Michelle. You'll be rewarded. Keep up the good work—oh, James mentioned something about a play this weekend, are you and Leron going?"

"...Yes."

"James and I are going to try and make it but he's rearranging the furniture and installing my new surround sound system this weekend, so I don't know for sure. Well, thanks again for your hard work. You're such a sweetheart, a real team player. I like that!" She waltzes out of the door.

"Chelle," Mrs. Feinstien buzzes, "Greg on four, do you want to take it?"

I slouch in my chair and sigh, "I guess so." This is going to be one of those days. "...Hello, Greg."

"What happened to you that Saturday? I waited and waited you never called. I was worried."

"I told you I was going to be busy. Besides, if you were so concerned you wouldn't be calling almost two weeks later."

"...I didn't think you wanted to hear from me, so I didn't call," his voice sounds guilty and deflated. He was right about that. I *didn't* want to hear from him. "How long is this going to go on? When are we going to see each other?"

"I'll call you when I'm ready. I'm trying to focus on other things." I raise my hand to look at my nails. I need to redo them.

"Focus on other things? What's more important than our future together?" he asks. Tired of the conversation running in circles, I tell him I'm not in the mood to talk. He demands we discuss it anyway. It's the same thing over and over again. I'm losing my patience and he knows it. "My mother's been asking about you, baby," he says, bringing up Mrs. Colbert, thinking it will get to me. She is one of the sweetest people I know. But bringing her up isn't going to work today.

"I have work to do."

"I don't understand you, woman." He raises his voice, "Do you know how hard it is to find a good, successful black man—you have one—and you're just kicking me aside? You're so touchy. It must be that time of the month—"

"Bye!" I hang up before he carries on. The day just started but Ann and Greg are already getting on my nerves! I need a chocolate donut.

▼

I calm down as the day progresses because I have lots of work to do. But I don't stay busy for long. Tonya stops by to say hello and that means I'll be running my mouth for at least ten or twenty minutes.

She takes a seat. "Why you lookin' like that?"

"I'm stressed. Ann is piling on the work. You know how she gets."

"Yeah, I'm glad she ain't my supervisor. I woulda told her 'bout herself a long time ago."

"I know. Normally I would've too, but I'm trying hard to get this promotion. My review is coming up and I need to stay on her good side."

"That doesn't mean you have to take her bull—"

Ann buzzes. "Michelle, when you get a moment, can you review the invoices from the Mobile Tron account? The accounting department says our numbers aren't matching theirs."

"Well, Mrs. Feinstein usually does th—"

"Yeah, I know, but I would feel more comfortable if you did it this time."

"Well, maybe she can—"

"Thanks, darling."

Tonya rolls her eyes as I bury my head in my hands. "This woman is driving me crazy. I know she's demanding, but she's never been like this."

"Like I said, I'm glad it ain't me!"

"To make matters worse, she's even dating Leron's best friend."

Tonya's eyes open wide as she puts both hands around her neck to make a choking gesture. "That's nasty I'm gonna throw up. He's sleeping with that fat heifer? I bet he puts a paper bag over her face before they bump uglies..."

"Girl, you're silly!"

" ...Probably cuts out lil' holes for her nose and mouth so she can breathe..." Tonya's bottom lips curls when I tell her Ann kept cutting her eyes at Leron. "You shoulda pulled them braids out her head and beat her wit'em!"

"Come on, you know that's not my style, Tee. Besides, I wouldn't embarrass Leron like that."

"Child, please! Ann disrespected *you like that*! You're too nice." Tonya gives me a ten minute 'if that was me, I would've did this and that' speech. When she finishes, I mention Greg called this morning.

She folds her arms and says, "I think you should give him a chance. You know he loves you. I wish my man treated me how Greg treats you."

"Tonya, why do you keep bugging me about this? I'm happy, let me be happy."

"I am. But sometimes you make quick decisions without thinkin' things through."

"Well not this time," I reply. Her eyes are full of concern. She is right about my tendency to act purely off of emotions. Sometimes I can get irrational. But this time, after looking at the situation from every possible angle, I think I'm doing the right thing.

Tonya gives me her two cents and leaves. I get back to sifting through the pile of papers on my desk. I glance at the days on my desk calendar. Two more days and the weekend will be here. It can't come soon enough.

▼

When Thursday comes, I'm on the borderline of being burnt out. Time is supposed to fly when you're busy, but my week is dragging. Ann took today off but she keeps calling in with more things for me to do. A blinking voicemail light greets me when I return from the cafeteria. Ann probably left another message with more orders. I haven't the slightest clue why she's been giving most of the work to me when her assistant does nothing but surf astrology websites all day. Maybe I should take it as a compliment! She must feel very confident in my abilities. That will be good when I have my job review. But half of the stuff she's giving me seems like busy work. She might be testing me. I ignore the blinking light for a few more minutes before checking the messages.

"You have three new messages and zero saved messages. First message today, 12:16 p.m.: Hey beautiful, it's Leron. I know Thursdays are your busiest days, but I wanna say hello. I'm thinking about you, and I can't wait to see you tomorrow night. Call me."

I smile after hearing his message. I'm looking forward to tomorrow night as well.

"...Second message recorded today, 12:21 p.m.: Michelle, it's Ann. Listen, I need you to start working on a proposal for the Edmington Electronics Group. If you could have most of it completed by next Monday, no later than Tuesday that would be great. We really need to get the ball rolling on this as soon as possible. Thanks, sweetheart—"

A day can't pass without her giving me more work. I knew it! Lord, please just let me make it through these next few weeks. I'm losing my mind!

"...Third message recorded today 12:33 p.m.: Hey baby, I guess you're at lunch or something. I'm sorry for the way I acted yesterday, give me call."

I knew Greg would call back. He is so predictable.

▼

Hours of sitting at a desk have my eyes feeling like soggy sandbags; my lower back aching; and my fingers cramping. It seems like the more work I finish, the more work I have to do. People have been stopping in every now and then to say 'bye', as they leave for the day. It's almost five-thirty but I probably won't leave until seven o'clock.

Tonya swings by on her way out. "Chelle, you still working? It's time to go," she says, peeking through the door.

"Yeah...I have a lot to do."

"I would keep you company, but David is leaving today. I gotta drop him off at the airport in a couple hours."

"How are you feeling? Are you okay?"

Clasping both hands in front of her, Tonya squeezes out a smile. "...Yeah, I'm fine. I'm gonna miss him, though. I really am."

"I know, Tee. But it'll all work out."

"I know it will. Besides, Gerald is calling me already!" She laughs. I playfully roll my eyes. "I'm teasing," she says. "I'm not even paying him any mind. Well, I gotta run, you know how traffic is."

Tonya loves David, but he runs the streets too much—he will have a field day out in California. All I can do is give her my support and wish for the best.

After she leaves, I get a Mountain Dew because I need something with a lot of caffeine. Massaging my eyes, I sit down to the computer. Soon as I began typing, I remember I need to return Leron's call from earlier. I drink half of my soda and gave him a ring.

"It's after five-thirty, what are you still doing at work?" he asks when I call.

"I know, but I have too much to get done. Media plans, proposals, invoices, there's just not enough time."

"Can you get your coworkers to help you out?"

"Ann pretty much wants me to do everything and then some! And

I don't want to seem incompetent. I'm up for a promotion soon—I don't want anything to interfere."

"Well, are we still on for the play tomorrow night or will you be too tired to go?"

I take another sip of soda. "We're definitely still on. I've been looking forward to it ever since you asked." Leron is the first man to ever ask me to a play. I've been asked to sporting events and concerts but no plays.

"You sure? I can go alone if you can't make it."

"Positive," I answer, picturing the smile on his face. "I'm going no matter what!"

"Now that's what I wanna hear! Do you know if Spurt and Anesia are going?" he asks.

"Ann's not sure. She mentioned something about putting in a sound system or something. They might be there, I don't know."

Leron is quiet for a moment. "...Uh...oh, really, a sound system?" he asks, stumbling over his words."...Oh, okay, w-well, sexy, I'ma let you finish doing what you gotta do."

"Okay, honey ."

"Call me if you need anything."

"You're so thoughtful, I will."

Our brief conversation makes my work a little more bearable, and that's good because I need to get as much done as possible. I will not be working late on Friday—that's for sure.

15

Soon as I hang up with Michelle, I start searching the top of my dresser looking for Anesia's number. I dial it quick and hard, hitting the keypads like they were the blame for everything. My unbuttoned work shirt flaps open and closed while I pace the living room holding the phone so tight, my hand is numb. Twisting and turning, my stomach feels like it's rising slowly up my throat. This freak has gone too far, I'm tired of this—enough is enough! When Anesia answers, my temples tighten and flinch, a burning knot forms in my chest.

"Well, well, well, Leron King, the ladies' man. Are you calling me because you miss me?"

"Yeah, like I miss a puss-filled cold sore! How'd you get my account information?"

"Oh, my, what on earth are you talking about?" she asks, playing dumb.

"Don't play stupid. You bought a surround sound system with my credit card!"

She lets out a short chuckle. "I see you've been talking to that whore, Michelle. What a big mouth she h—"

"Answer me!"

"Oh, calm down, Leron! We wouldn't want you to get a hernia from all that yelling, now would we?" Her voice sounds evil and condescending, speaking to me like I'm a snotty-nosed schoolboy.

"How did you get my information?"

"You're such an idiot—no brains with that sexy body of yours. I'll bet you'd be surprised at what kind of things people throw in the trash: old frozen food boxes, empty fruit punch jugs...bank and credit card statements." She laughs. "You made everything so easy, Leron."

"I'm pressing charges. You can rummage through all the trash you want in jail."

"You can't prove anything. Everything is in your name. I simply used your account and had it shipped to another location; then I had that strong James go pick it up. He's so helpful."

I march from the living room to the dining room and back. "You won't get away with this. Trust me!"

"Oh, shut up! You wouldn't have even figured it out if it weren't for that blabbermouth Michelle. That girl is working so hard you'll have to forgive her. The poor child isn't in her right mind. She's too concerned about a silly promotion she won't get. Being the boss is lovely."

"You can do whatever you want to me but don't involve Michelle and Spurt," I say, pointing in air like I'm pointing directly at Anesia.

"Oh, I get it, now you want to be noble? Too late! All you had to do was treat me with respect and common courtesy."

"I told you I—"

"Bye, bye."

I can't believe she's doing all this over a silly misunderstanding. And I hate that people I care about are caught in the middle. If I tell them what's going on, I might lose them. If I don't tell them, I still might lose them. My fate lies in the hands of some crazed psycho maniac. And it doesn't feel good. I hope she's not at the play tomorrow night. I wanna just relax and enjoy myself without worrying if she gonna do something crazy.

▼

Friday afternoon, I made sure to finish my appointments faster than usual. I gotta fresh haircut on my lunch break and I picked up my favorite silk shirt from the cleaners. Everything is set for tonight except Michelle. It's an hour before the play, and I haven't heard from her. I've been calling every fifteen minutes and all I get is voicemail. I can't help getting a lil' nervous, something's gotta be wrong. She always returns my phone calls.

Another fifteen minutes pass. I'm chillin', waiting on the couch fully-dressed and ready to go. I call again.

"You've reached Michelle Barkley sorry I can't come to the—" I hang up and I try her at work. Anesia probably has her staying late again.

"Michelle speaking."

"Hey baby, is everything all right? I've been calling your house and your cell for the last two hours."

"Oh, I'm sorry. I haven't gone home yet and I turned my cell phone off so I could concentrate." She exhales into the phone, "...Go ahead without me. I'll meet you there because I have a little more work to finish. Then I have to go home, freshen up and then I—"

"I'll wait for you."

"No, honey, go ahead without me."

"No, I'll wait for you, I want you to come."

She stops typing to think. "You know what, I'm going to wrap this up in a minute, my brain is fried anyway. By the time you make it to my house, I'll be there waiting."

▼

We make it to the theatre towards the end of the first act. People are dressed in suits and gowns and almost every seat is filled. An usher manages to find us two in the back. I see Dave, X and Lisa sitting near the front, but I don't see Spurt and Anesia—thank goodness. I don't need *two* tragedies in one night. I keep expecting Anesia any minute. My neck jerks every time someone walks down the aisle. That's making it hard to watch Ra. He doesn't even look like himself on stage. He's wearing black tights and his hair isn't slicked back like usual. He's playing a very convincing Romeo. Michelle is paying close attention to his every word. I'm trying to do the same but too many thoughts are going through my mind. I've been on edge since that crazy dinner date. My life got so much drama I should be up there performing with Ra'ed. I kiss Michelle's hand to soothe my nerves. She smiles, eyes glistening like two big brown rubies. I feel slightly better.

Ra is doing good for his acting debut—he hasn't forgotten any lines! Maybe acting is his true calling. The play is cool—long, but cool. Michelle seems to be enjoying herself so I'm happy. I don't let go of her hand until the final curtain falls. I had a nice time. Once I realized Anesia wasn't coming, my nerves settled. After the play, we congratulate Ra, chat with X, Lisa, and Dave, then head to Michelle's place to unwind.

▼

Miles Davis' *Birth of Cool* spins low in the background. I'm sitting on the sofa tapping my leg to the rhythm, waiting for Michelle to change. The television is off, the lights are dim, and everything feels peaceful here. Soon, Michelle sashays in front of me.

"Finished," she says, modeling a baby blue satin nightgown with matching fuzzy slippers. "Which outfit do you like better: this one or the one I wore to the play?"

I take her hand and pull her into my lap. "Well, let's see. I think I like this one 'cause of the cute fuzzy slippers."

She sticks her feet out and examines them. With both arms around my neck, she says in a grumpy girlish voice, "Don't be picking on my fuzzy wuzzy slippers."

"I'm not. They're cute."

She kisses my nose. "You better say that if you know what's good for you, Mister!"

I chuckle. "You got some big ol' feet, though!"

"I do not!"

"Yeah you do. Look at them gators! You know what they say about women with big feet, right?"

She waves her small fist in my face. "What?"

"They have big shoes!"

We laugh.

"You're so crazy."

"Crazy about you." I place my arm around her and kiss her lips, "So how did you like the play, baby? Did you have a nice time?"

"I loved it. That was the first play I've ever gone to—except for my little niece's Christmas play. I had a great time, thanks for inviting me."

"It was my first real play too. An Indian Romeo and an Asian Juliet...Shakespeare's probably turning in his grave right now."

"Awww, I thought it was cute. Your friend was good."

"You think so? I'll tell him you said—what's that smell?" I catch whiff of a vanilla scent.

"It's a new lotion I'm trying. You like it?"

Pulling her closer, I inhale the fragrance. "Mmm, girl, you smell delicious! If we are what we eat, then I could be you by morning time!"

She shifts her weight and smiles. Looking deep in my eyes, she presses her forehead against mine. "How do you always know the right things to say and when to say them?"

I kiss beneath her neck and I reply, "I dunno. I just say what I feel. But right now, my heart and soul is doing the talking, not me."

She stands and takes me by the hand. "Come here, I have something I want you to see."

I follow her down the hall like an anxious puppy about to get a table-food meal instead of regular dog chow. But I still find it hard to read her. I can't tell if she wants to make love or just show me another poem or something. It doesn't even matter, though. I'm getting excited just from having a beautiful half-dressed woman lead me to her bedroom. The room smells like her and everything is in place; the perfume bottles on the dresser are in line; and the burgundy bedspread is drawn back in a perfect triangle.

Standing in front of the bed I ask, "What is it? What do you want me to see, baby?"

"This." With a seductive smile, her nightgown falls to the floor like a downy feather floating to the ground. She stands naked and magnificent as a Swahili sculpture. Her body outshines the small lamp on the nightstand. "Do you like what you see?" she asks, noticing my satisfaction.

"I *like* what I *see*, and I'm gonna *love* what I *touch*... but actions speak louder than words, so I won't say anything else." I kiss her on the neck. She raises her chin higher wanting me to continue. Kissing slowly down the right side and even slower down the left, my sporadic breaths bounce off her skin, carrying her scent deep into my nostrils.

She pulls me closer by the inside front of my pants. Her warm chest heats my silk shirt. And I know she feels me pressing hard against her. Our lips briefly entangle before she pulls back. Throbbing and pulsating with anticipation, I loosen my belt, gazing into her starved eyes. Grabbing me again, she slaps my hands away, unbuckling the belt herself. Two blinks later, my silk shirt, khakis, and boxer shorts are on the floor. In a graceful swoop, I lift her into my arms, gently placing her on the bed. Pulling back her hair, I nibble on her exposed earlobes.

"...O Romeo, Romeo! wherefore art thou Romeo?" She smiles and moans, sensually raking her fingers across my back.

"Here," I whisper, kissing her firm left nipple. "...And here," I kiss the right. "...And here...and here...and here..." Her hand guides my head while I continue down the middle of her stomach, tasting the fine line of hair from navel to waistline. Arching her back, she quivers each time my hot tongue touches her. Watching the quick rising and falling of her abdomen makes me anxious. But I have to be patient; each move has to be on point. Precise. She's not a chick I met at a smoky nightclub, she's Michelle Barkley—a woman I have real feelings for.

She motions me to lie down beneath her. Before my head hits the pillow, she kisses me; inhales me. Her aggressiveness catches me by surprise, but I don't mind. She gets a condom outta the nightstand drawer and holds my manhood, stroking it from its base, the neck, and tip as it jerks from the sensation. Once fitted, she pushes it inside her sparkling gem, churning forward and back, side-to-side, controlling the deepness. Biting her bottom lip, with each intense stroke, she grips my shoulders while circling my chest with wet kisses. Every time I try to roll over and take charge, she resists until *she's* ready.

She's on her back now with outstretched arms welcoming me on top. I enter—quickly pull out—then enter again, teasing her with my solid thickness. Gripping my waist, she drives me deeper in the chamber walls. Mouth open wide, I can't help breathing outta control. My reactions turn her on and she takes my face into her hands, kissing me sloppier than before. I keep rhythm, steadily stroking the sweet spot; squeezing her nipples between my lips, licking them well; and loving her soft hands moving along the muscular grooves of my arms.

Rolling over, resting her head at the bed's end, she waits to feel me from behind. Occasionally, I kiss her back, licking the sweat from my lips. Massaging her shoulders with one hand, and breasts with the other, I give her my love smoothly. Several times she looks back to see my facial expressions but I don't have to say much—she knows it's good. I know it's the bomb.

My grunts turn to groans; her moans become screams. Now I'm pushing harder and faster using the side of the bed for leverage. Together we move like twin synchronized swimmers fluttering in and outta the water. I can...I can feel the muscles tightening below. Closing my eyes, I lean my head back, and then forward again trying to resist—trying to hold on a lil' longer. I'm...really... struggling to make it last but she has other ideas. Working her body in quick circular motions, she rocks back hard—then we lose it—our muscles squeeze and release. Lord have mercy.

16

Tonya has my den smelling like tortilla chips and salsa. I don't think she realizes how loud she's chewing either. Whenever a tortilla crumb falls on the sofa cushion, she picks it up and stuffs it in her mouth all in one motion. She chomps away asking me question after question. We didn't speak much over the weekend and I knew she would make a big deal about it.

"...Girl, how come lately every time I call, you don't answer the phone?"

"I told you Leron and I were going to see his friend in Romeo and Juliet."

"How was it?"

"I had a marvelous time. It was nice doing something different for a change. And it sure beat sitting around like Greg and I did all the time."

"Chelle, tell me something," her voice lowers. "All this time you been spending with him and you ain't got your freak on?" she asks, waving a tortilla chip as she talks. I smile inside without answering her. "Hello, did you hear me? Have you guys done the horizontal monkey dance or what?"

"...Well—"

"Wait a minute! You did it didn't you?"

I can't stop giggling. "Well, we—"

"You did! You did! You did! You wild girl, you! Chelle, Chelle got her some, eieioooh, with a bang, bang here and an ugh, ugh there, eieioooh," she bounces on the sofa, singing to the tune of *Old McDonald*.

I almost choke from laughing at her ghetto remix. "You are a trip!"

"I thought you knew. So now, how was it?"

"...I don't know where to start."

"Well, just start, girl. Hurry up, I'm curious—horny minds wanna know!" She licks salsa from her fingers.

"Okay, after the play, we went back to my house to relax..."

"Yeah? Keep going."

"We listened to jazz music, talked some, joked around—you know, just having fun and everything..."

"Girl, will you hurry up and get to the juicy stuff?" Whenever sex is the topic, Tonya always gets overly excited and attentive.

"Okay, okay, don't rush me. You know I don't talk about these things as freely as you do."

After I tell her what happened, she smiles uncontrollably. "What's gotten into you? I never knew you were a lil' freak!"

I know she's only teasing, but I don't like the sound of 'freak.' "I'm not! This isn't like me at all. I don't know, I just feel bold and daring around him."

"Yeah, bold, daring, and freaky! So was it good?"

"Tonya, you know I don't like to talk about all that!"

"Girl, it's me. You know a sister gots to know!"

"If you must know, then yes—he was very sensual and passionate—and besides, anything is better than what I've been getting—which is nothing!"

"Sensual and passionate? I don't care about all that, was he packin' or not?" Even though I know how Tonya is, some of the things she says still shock me.

"I can't believe you just asked me—yeah I can." I mumble, "Yes, he was...well-endowed if that's what you're asking, Tonya."

"Mmm. Go on wit' yo undercover freaky deaky self. I gotta meet Mr. Leron. I wanna see who turned my girl out!"

I roll my neck in a sassy, playful way. "Too bad you'll be gone by the time he comes over."

"I can stay longer."

I shake my head 'no.' I know how flirtatious she is. I don't want her making Leron uncomfortable. But I know she won't leave me alone until I give in. To spare myself a headache, I tell her she can stay long enough to say a quick hello, nice to met you, and then she has to leave.

"Okay, okay, girl. You act like I'ma bite him or something." she says.

"Who are you trying to fool? Tee, you know you like biting men!" I joke. She puts a finger to her lips as if to say, 'shhh, don't tell the secret.'

We laugh.

▼

Tonya's face lights up when Leron knocks at the door. He kisses me and walks inside. I never knew a plain, white muscle shirt and black jeans could look so sexy.

"Honey, this is my best friend, Tonya."

"Hello."

"Tonya, this is Leron."

"It's very, very, nice to meet you. I've heard good things about you," Tonya slyly looks at Leron's pants, using her ghetto x-ray vision to see inside. "...so many good things."

"Tonya was just leaving, right Tonya?" I stop her before she can say anything crude.

"...Yeah..." She sticks out her bottom lip, gets her things, and walks to the door. "See ya, Chelle. Byeeee, Leron." Her tone livens, "Hope to see you s—" I shut the door.

"Sorry about that. Tonya is something else." I move the tortilla chip bag off of the sofa before Leron sits down, "But I love her to death! That's my girl."

"It's cool. How was your day, baby?" he asks.

"Pretty busy for a Monday. The phone wouldn't stop ringing, my computer kept crashing, and my neck is sore from looking at client files all day."

"We can't have that, now can we?" He gently reaches behind my neck, rotating his fingers in semicircles. "Does this help?"

All of my body loosens from his touch. "...Mmmmm, just a little," I moan.

He smiles. "Just a lil', huh? What if we did this naked?" The deviousness in his voice turns me on as much as his words. He knows my answer without it ever leaving my lips. We float down the hall to the bedroom.

▼

Leron's naked body presses against my back as he stands behind me. "Just lay down and relax," he whispers, hot breath brushing my earlobe. I lie down on my stomach, resting my arms underneath the pillow. I feel his length bulging between his warm thighs as he straddles me, sliding both palms down my back. "I call this the Leron special," he says, massaging my shoulders.

"Mmmmm, Leron special," I mumble, eyes closed, head turned sideways.

"...It uh...it helps promotes the proper movement of your body's energy..."

"I have no clue what you're talking about, but it sounds like you know what you're doing..."

"I know a lil' something, something," he says. "The secret is all in the fingers. You gotta know how to use your fingers..."

"Mmm. All in...the...fingers..." Whatever he's doing is very relaxing. I can fall asleep any m...minute.

The phone rings. I reach to the nightstand and answer.

"WHERE ARE YOU, MICHELLE?" Ann yells. "We're presenting a campaign in ten minutes!"

I gasp. "I'm sorry. I'm so, so sorry. It totally slipped my mind. I'll be there quick as I can, Ann."

"Michelle, this is completely unacceptable. Unacceptable! Do you hear me?"

Leron taps my arm. "Do you hear me?" he asks. "Michelle...you hear me?"

"Huh?"

I lift my head from the pillow. "Oh no! I'm late for work!"

"What are you talking about, baby? It's ten o'clock at night."

"Oh..." Slightly embarrassed, I come to my senses. I know I've been working too hard when I start dreaming about my job. I'm losing it.

Leron strokes the top of my head. "I guess you dozed off for a minute," he says, running a finger down my leg. "...I was asking if you were ready for a *full body* massage."

I turn on my back and smile as he moves his body on mine. "I'm ready, baby."

17

There's a Thursday night NBA double-header on and I'm gonna watch both games. I leave for New Hampshire tomorrow and I know I won't have time to watch any ball up there. I'm relaxing on the couch, glancing at the pre-game show, and talking to Femia. I just told her that Romeo and Juliet was tight since psycho Anesia didn't come. I make sure not to mention what happened after the play. I don't wanna tell her, not yet. Femia doesn't believe in premarital sex—she'll drill me—probably worse than she did when I told her I slept with Anesia. All she could say then was, "You used one pick-up line too many." But I'm done with all that. I haven't messed with any other chicks since meeting Michelle—she could be *the one*.

"Uh oh, here we go again," Femia groans, "Didn't you say the same thing about Keyoni and what about Desiree?"

I knew she would bring them up. They were my eighth and ninth grade girlfriends who dumped me for "bad boys." I used to write Femia every other week for advice. I was just a young buck, didn't know much about chicks then.

"You're always bringing them up. That was kiddy stuff—this is the—"

"Real thing," she interrupts, finishing the sentence before I can. We've had this exact conversation several times and I understand why she doesn't believe me. But this time is much different. Really! She says that this doesn't necessarily mean that Michelle is *the one* for me and that if things don't work out, I could be hurt bad. I rationalize by saying that's just a part of life.

"I can't go around bottling up my feelings inside like some people do."

Femia gotta lil' defensive when I said that. Judging from her tone, she thinks that's a cheap shot at her. Realizing I mean nothing by it, she pauses a second and says go for it. She still sounds unconvinced—but oh well.

"Hey, two more days and you'll be done with school!" I change the subject.

"Yes Lord, hallelujah!"

"I hope you're not gonna try and make me pack all your stuff. I'm coming up there to have fun—not to work!" I helped move her stuff to the dorms her freshman year. All she did was supervise while me and her father did all the work—at least she fed me good. I kinda wish she would've gone to school outta state, see other places, do other things. But she's close to her family and loves being around them. When she said she was moving all the way to Texas to work, I was happy and surprised at the same time.

▼

I pack my things and begin printing out the rough draft of my book early the next morning. With folded arms, I watch the printer spit out each page. Holding the thick stack of paper like a father holds a newborn son, I flip through the pages and smile. Most of it probably stinks—but it's mine. I thought I'd be a lil' more hyped but I guess too many things have been happening to fully absorb the satisfaction. Maybe going back up North will clear my mind.

Michelle pulls up out front and honks the horn. I told her I'd just take MARTA to the airport but she insisted on taking me herself. Grabbing my bags, I rush outta the door, sling my luggage in the backseat, and hop in. I don't wanna mention anything about my book yet 'cause I wanna have time to celebrate with her. I plan on surprising her when I get back.

"Hey, sexy lady! Are you smiling at me or is the sun coming out?"

She looks at me and winks. "Both! Now fasten your seat belt, you know my rules."

I chuckle.

"So are you excited?" she asks.

"Yeah. Every time I go back home, I get excited. There's something special about going back to where you grew up. But I'ma be just as excited to come back to see you."

"Yeah, sure you will. You're going to forget all about me while you're up there."

I lean over to kiss her cheek. "I doubt that. I'm missing you already, and I'm still in Atlanta."

Michelle's mood changes as we near the airport. She doesn't laugh or smile as much. And all her answers to my questions are short and to the point. I ask if she's feeling okay.

She checks the rearview mirror and changes lanes before answering.

"I find out about my promotion today and I'm nervous. Recently we had a new senior vice-president transfer to our office from Chicago, and he's not familiar with my work."

I slowly nod my head. "Oh, I see." I forgot today is her performance review.

"But Ann's doing the actual review; I work with her everyday and she knows my abilities—so that's good." Now, *my* mood changes. I feel real guilty right about now 'cause I'm the reason she might not get promoted.

Half of me wants to tell her everything right now and the other half is fighting it. Maybe I should just wait and see what happens first. A dry lump slithers down my throat as the words "Well, I know you'll get it, baby" leave my mouth.

"I hope so. Then we'll celebrate when you get back," she replies.

"How about you pull over to the side of the road and we celebrate right now?"

"You wish."

"I sure do," I say with a mischievous smile.

She waits a few minutes then looks at me and asks if Femia is an old girlfriend. I can see where she's headed with her question. But I let her know from the start that Femia is just a childhood buddy. My mother used to babysit her.

"Is she pretty?" she asks.

I laugh to myself. I'm not falling for this trick question. If I say 'yes,' I'll be in hot water. If I said 'no' she'll think I'm lying—I lose all the way around. I know what I'ma say. "She looks okay, but she's no Michelle Barkley." That's the safest answer I know. Michelle nods even though she's not satisfied. It's cool; at least I dodged a bullet. "I get back on Sunday night at seven-thirty, you're gonna be able to pick me up?"

"Of course."

Since Michelle was so inquisitive about Femia, I figure it's the perfect time to ask about Greg.

"You heard from Greg?"

She cuts her eyes at me. Taking a deep breath, she answers, "He calls from time to time to see what I'm up to. You know how men are when they realize they've lost something good—they desperately try to get it back by making a million promises."

"Well, I already know what I have," I pat her thigh as flashes from the night of the play come to mind. "Does he know about me? About us?"

Michelle exits the Georgia 400 and merges on to I-75 South, cutting in front of a Volkswagen Bug. "No, honey, I haven't told him yet."

I roll my tongue around in my mouth and stare at the road. All this time and he still doesn't know about me? I take my hand from her thigh to scratch my head. "I understand, and that's all cool but I'ma let you know, I don't wanna be second. I've been the *other* guy before, and I ain't doing it again."

"Don't worry, you're *the* guy, things are just fragile right now—timing is crucial."

"Okay then, while I'm gone these few days, you can let him know the deal."

"I'll talk to him." She places a hand on my knee, "Everything will be fine by the time you get back."

I lean against the headrest and think to myself, *it better be.*

18

Today is the big day. I'll find out about my promotion and how much money comes with it! After dropping Leron off at the airport, I drive to work; my review was scheduled for 11:30 a.m. My watch says 11:49 a.m. I'm waiting in my office anxious and nervous wondering what's taking so long. What are they doing in there? Something must be wrong. I buzz Mrs. Feinstein.

"Yes, sweetie?"

"What are they up to in there? They were supposed to call me in at 11:30."

"I'm not sure hon'. They've been in there almost forty-five minutes."

"I just want to get this over with so I can relax. Okay, I'll just keep waiting."

During my third game of computer solitaire, Mr. Bill Ellicott, our new senior vice-president, calls me. His office is dull, impersonal with few decorations and no pictures—except for one on the bookshelf of him and another man. The scent of Mr. Ellicott's strong cologne mixed with the smell of Ann's banana strawberry smoothie is nauseating.

"How are you today, Michelle?" he asks, loosely shaking my hand.

"I'm doing fine, sir. And yourself?"

"I can't complain—even if I did, it wouldn't change anything!" His mousy features stretch when he laughs.

Ann is sitting to the side, holding a manila folder and a notepad. "We're sorry for starting so late," she says. "We were going over some figures and lost track of time."

"No problem."

Adjusting his tie, Mr. Ellicott's tired eyes peer at mine. "Great, make yourself at home; let's get started. First of all, I want to apologize for not getting to know you all as fast as I would've liked. It's been very hectic around here as you can imagine. But Ann has worked closely with you on a daily basis. With that in mind, I'll just sit back and let her lead the review..."

"Okay, Michelle, here's your employee assessment—here's a copy for you, Bill. You'll notice each item is rated on a scale of one to seven, one being unsatisfactory, seven being exceptional. As I read each assessment, feel free to comment and ask questions.

"Item one. Understands job duties and responsibilities: Michelle understands and performs her duties and responsibilities well. She knows the importance of superb account maintenance; understands every aspect of the ad production process; and asks questions if instructions are unclear..." I look at my score and see they gave me six for that one. I guess that's okay.

"...Item two. Neatness, thoroughness, and accuracy of work

performed: Michelle is extremely organized and her work is always accurate and thorough..." Good! They gave me a seven, on that one. That's more like it.

As we continue, the review seems fair. I would've worded some things differently, but for the most part, I'm satisfied. With every item discussed, I become more confident about the promotion. But when Ann reads the last section, my confidence deflates to a weak fizzle: "...In addition to areas previously discussed, describe areas where employee's performance can be improved..." Sitting the review in her lap, Ann sighs and says, "You do great work, Michelle. You're quick, well organized, and clients love you. However, some areas could use improving. For one, I feel you could take on a little more responsibility with projects..."

Did she just say I need to take on more responsibility? I've been doing the workload of three people! "I'd like to make a comment please."

"Sure."

"I'm confused. I've taken a lot of responsibility for my work and I often help others with theirs."

"You're right, as of late you *have* been taking on more responsibilities." *As of late? Heifer, I've been working like a slave since I started here two years ago!* I think to myself. "...But overall you could take on more initiative. Let's see...oh, you could also work on meeting deadlines in a timely manner..."

"Meeting deadlines in a timely manner? I usually complete projects far in advance and I've never missed a deadline," I defend myself.

Ann glances at her notepad. "Well, just recently I asked a client for an extension because you didn't complete their media plans on time."

"Wait a minute! I had those plans ready—you told me you didn't need them anymore. Remember I came in early and finished?" She's playing stupid with me now?

"Hmm. I don't recall that, maybe we had a communication breakdown. Your commitment and dedication could use improvement too. When the clock strikes 5:00 p.m., you shutdown and rarely stay later."

I scoot forward to the edge of my seat. "That's not true. I work late at least three times a week because I don't like carrying unfinished work into the next day..."

Ann then says she never sees me. But that's because she works on the other side of the building. Besides, she always sneaks out around four-thirty. She taps her ballpoint pen on the pad, pointing to another comment. "...Another thing I've noticed is how you use your time on slow days. I think you should be more constructive. Many times, I've passed your office and noticed you joking around with coworkers or talking on the phone with friends. There are better ways to use your time..."

I scoot back in the chair. "Yes, I do take short breaks sometimes, just like everyone else—"

"Being an Associate Account Supervisor is very demanding, Michelle—to be honest with you, I don't feel comfortable placing you in that role just yet. But we'll work on strengthening your skills to get you to the next level. In six months we'll assess your performance again and reconsider you for the position."

"I'm the top Account Manager here, I know what I'm capable of and you do too—I can do this job, Ann!"

"I know you're talented, but I don't want to prematurely place you in a position you're not ready for. But I want to stress the fact that you're doing a fantastic job, keep up the good work! Mr. Ellicott do you have anything to add?" I look at Mr. Elliot and frown. *He doesn't even know what's going on. What can he possibly say?* I wonder as he leans forward to speak.

"Michelle, you strike me as being very smart and ambitious; I don't want you to be disappointed. I first joined this company as an intern... gradually, I worked my way up to Senior Vice President— and I wasn't half as bright as you! You'll be an Associate Account Supervisor in no time."

▼

The door swings wide when I storm into the ladies room. There isn't anyone inside, but I don't care either way...*To be honest with you, I don't feel comfortable placing you in that role,* those deafening words seem to bounce off the restroom walls, taunting me while I dry my eyes in the mirror. "Come on now, Michelle, get it together," I whisper to myself. "You have to get through the rest of the day." ...*We'll work on strengthening your skills to get you to the next level...* "I know this job inside and out." ...*But I want to stress that you're doing a fantastic job, keep up the good work...* "I must not be doing enough; I didn't get promo—" Ann walks in. I act like I don't see her.

"Michelle? Michelle, I hope you don't take this review personal. It's all business—nothing more. I—"

"You sure made it sound *personal*! Why did you sit in front of his face and lie? You know good and well I do excellent work."

"I *didn't* lie! Some of my facts were just a little...fuzzy, that's all..." *Fuzzy like the hair growing out of that nasty mole on your face? I* mumble in my mind. "Don't be so uptight, you'll get the silly job in six months."

"That's six months longer than I want to wait."

Ann steps closer with a hand on her hip. "You really don't have a choice!"

"I don't understand you. All year I've been hearing how good of a job I've been doing, how I'll be rewarded; and then you take away everything I've worked for?" I look in directly in her face. "If you have a problem with me, we need to fix it right here, right now!"

"I don't like your tone of voice," she says, folding her arms.

"I don't care what you like!"

"...Okay. You want to know the problem? I'll tell you the problem." Her hands drop back to her hips, "The problem is I really don't like you—never have, never will—that's the problem! And since I'm the boss, there's nothing you can do about it!"

"...I should slap that crooked-teeth grin off your face, but I don't want to get my hand dirty! But don't think this is over Ann, because it's not. Now get out of my way, I've looked at you too long—I'm going home sick!"

"You got that right, it's not over! IT'S NOT OVER, MICHELLE," she yells as I walk out.

▼

Walking through the parking garage to my car, I make a U-turn towards Ann's red 325i BMW. My conscience seesaws back and forth: *DON'T DO IT Michelle, what if you get caught? DO IT Michelle, who cares if you get caught, things can't get any worse!* I look to the left. Right. Nobody is watching. But I'm still hesitant. I still hear Ann in my head: *You want to know the problem. I'll tell you the problem. The problem is I really don't like you—never have, never will—that's the problem! And since I'm the boss, there's nothing you can do about it!* Her words supply the fuel I need. Holding my keys tight, I glance the parking garage again to make sure no one sees me. I casually scrape deep and hard, keying the entire left side of her car—and smile while doing it. I feel slightly better but most of the hurt, anger, and disappointment remain like the scratches in her paint. I take a step back to admire my work, smile, and walk to my car.

▼

My tires squeal when I speed out of the parking garage. I'm going to Lennox Square mall, then Phipps mall after that, to temporarily shop away my worries. As I turn left on Peachtree Dunwoody Road, my cell phone rings. The caller ID displays the office number and I hesitate before answering.

"...Michelle, speaking."

"Since you hate me anyway, I might as well come clean."

"What are you talking about, Ann?"

"I've been sleeping with Leron for the past month. That's what I'm talking about!"

I push the phone tighter to my ear. "WHAT?"

"You heard me! I feel so guilty knowing I took your man, so tell him we're through..."

"HA! You're funny!"

"If you think I'm joking that's your problem. But I'm sure going to miss his sexy body and that cute birthmark on his right butt cheek...mmm!" I pull the phone away from my ear. *How does she know about his*—a driver honking his horn interrupts my thought. I lost focus of everything for a moment and didn't notice the traffic light had turned green. I gather myself, slowly returning the phone to my ear. "...He's just like the rest of them...A DOG! By the way, I need you to come in early Monday morning, I'll think of *something* for you to do. Have a nice weekend!" Ann laughs.

I don't know what to think or feel. Just when I think things can't get any worse...they do. My face tightens, turning cold then hot. Tears fall fast. As I wipe my watery eyes, my heart slides to the pit of my stomach; and every driver passing by seems to stare. "This is too much." I scream, slamming my hand on the steering wheel, "TOO MUCH!" Thinking of Leron's lies makes the tears fall even faster: *And listening to your words and watching you say them captivated me*—what a big liar! I thought Leron and I had something special, I really did. I just knew he was sincere and honest but it was just an act—an act I fell for. Tonya's voice floats in my head, *Leron probably just another SP anyway; You know, men who gotta line for everything and swear they're God's gift to women.* How could I've been so naive and silly? I had no clue about anything. That fat, nasty, backstabbing—I should've known. I should've known.

I almost blame myself for everything. But I realize it's not my fault. Even still, I feel horrible and my head aches. My cell phone rings again as I fumble through my purse for Advil. If this is Ann again I'm going to—oh, what's Greg calling for? Before answering, I clear my throat. I don't want to sound like I've been crying.

"Hey, sugar, I know you don't like me calling your work number, so I called your cell. I'm off today and I've been sitting here thinking about you. How are things going?"

"You don't want to know..."

"Sure I do—hey, have you been crying?" This is just great, he can tell. "What's wrong?"

I sniff and sigh, "I had my review today..."

"I take it you didn't get the position you wanted."

"Nope, Ann doesn't think I'm ready."

"That's ridiculous! You work harder than anybody there. How can she think that?"

"I wanted to know the same thing so I confronted her; we had a heated argument; she threatened me, I threatened her; I left early, and then—"

"Whoa, Whoa, Whoa. Slow down. You guys threatened each other?"

"It's a long story..." I sniffle.

"Where are you?"

"Georgia 400, on my way to Lennox."

"Why don't you come over and tell me the whole story? We'll relax, grab a bite to eat and see if we can cheer you up. I've been acting like a fool lately and I want to make things right."

"I-I don't know about th—"

"Come on, I want to hear everything, and you know I want to see you. When you're ready to leave, you can leave—I won't try and make you stay," he says.

A while back, something like this happened. It was the first week Greg's company landed that big contract. One evening he was supposed to pick me up from work and take me out for a romantic night. He didn't even call to let me know the meeting would last longer than he thought. I was standing outside the office building waiting. Tonya had left already so, Mrs. Feinstein, bless her heart, waited with me almost an hour before taking me home. Greg claimed he wasn't able to leave the conference room to call me. I was upset for days, told him I didn't want to speak to him anytime soon. Two days later, I was depressed about losing a client. Greg called out of the blue and convinced me to come over. Before I knew it, I was naked, covered in scented oils.

"That's not a good idea, Greg but I'll call you when I get back from the mall."

"...At least tell me you'll think about it?"

"Fine... I'll think about it."

▼

After my wild shopping binge, I'm now the new owner of two dresses, six pairs of shoes, two bottles of perfume, a leather coat—it's summertime but it was on sale, and one high credit card bill coming next month. The salespeople were happy to see me come and sad to see me go. Single-handedly I probably helped them get a pay raise. Shopping served its purpose. I was so busy going from store to store, trying on things, looking for sales, that I hardly thought about my job, Ann or Leron. Now that I'm back in my car, everything is resurfacing.

Exhaust fumes mixed with stale air whips in my face when I roll down the window and pull up to the Georgia 400 toll plaza. As I move closer to the booth, I glance at all of the shopping bags in the backseat as if they have the answers to my questions. Why is this happening to me? What have I done to deserve any of this? Ann's been sleeping with Leron and just salivating for a chance to rub it in my face. And then Leron, Mr. 'my heart and soul is doing the talking, not me'—I can't get over it, he played me well. For all I know he's probably in New Hampshire seducing his so-called friend too while I'm here alone and hurt. Two can play that game. I think I'll have a little fun of my own.

▼

Greg answers the door with a shocked expression even though I called on the way over and agreed to have dinner with him.

167

"You look surprised," my voice trails off. As I walk inside, I'm met by a raspberry fragrance that smells like it was sprayed seconds before I arrived.

"Well, I thought you would change your mind. That's been happening a lot these days."

I give him a nasty look to let him know I don't appreciate the snide remark. He quickly offers an apology followed by a quick kiss on the cheek. His lips feel unusual against my skin, like they don't belong.

He sits beside me on a big velvet sofa in the living room. "I miss you so much. You don't know how happy I am to see you. I constantly think about you, what you're doing, how things are going..."

Well, I was doing great, having the best time I've had in a while until everything collapsed today, I think to myself. The man who quickly stole my heart isn't the caring, sensitive, honest person I made him out to be. When I told Leron I would tell Greg about him, I meant it—no need for that now. And I owe a special thanks to my fake, backstabbing supervisor for helping to ruin my relationship with him—not to mention screwing me over at work.

Greg and I order carryout Italian food and drive back to his house to eat. I make sure to keep our conversation light the entire time. We talk about general things like world events, music, and even did some reminiscing—which makes both of us laugh plenty of times. That's good. It's helping to ease my mind temporarily even though I've been drifting in and out of the conversation. But every time I think about how bad today has been, the more appealing Greg becomes.

He takes a sip of wine and slowly sits the glass on the table.

"...After you said you were going shopping, I ran out and did some shopping of my own, and I got you something," he says, smiling.

"You got me something?"

He stands and grabs my hand. "...It's in the room." I look at him slyly, acknowledging the blatant attempt to get me in the bedroom. I laugh to myself because I did the same thing with Leron. "Oh, I bet you think I'm just trying to get you in bed?" he asks, as if reading my mind. "Fine, I'll stay here, you go look." He sits down. "Go ahead, baby."

Curiosity is getting the best of me. Besides, anything that will make me feel better is fine with me. "Okay." I stand up slowly and walk to the bedroom. Except for the white bedroom walls and evergreen pillows cases, everything is black. Stacked on the dresser next to his laptop are C++, Linux, and XML computer programming manuals. I walk over to a humongous pink bag sitting in the center of the bed and peep inside.

"Greeeeeeg!" I pull out a giant stuffed Panda bear. "It's adorable..."

Greg walks in the room with a smile. "I figured your other Panda might want some company." A few months back, I saw the same panda bear in an imports store at the mall. It was handmade in China and very expensive. Greg said only a fool would pay that much for a "toy."

I squeeze the bear in my arms and smile. "I guess you're a fool."

"Guess so. I can't help it, I'll do anything for you because it's the little things that matter the most, right?" He steps closer and stops at the sight of my uneasy expression. I respond with a partial smile because I'm not exactly sure how to reply. "Uh...there's something else in there," he says in a shaky low voice, pointing to the bag.

Glad the awkward moment passed, I take a deep breath. "More?" I sit down, put the bag on the floor, and look inside again. Sitting in the bottom is a small red box with a yellow bow. I glance at Greg. He looks more excited than I do. My mouth hangs wide open after opening the box. "Ohhhh...Ohhhh," are the only words I can say. I look at Greg again, then the box. Greg. The box. Inside is a picture of us at Zoo Atlanta—the first picture we'd ever taken together. It's only a snapshot but it's my favorite by far. His arm is around me and I have my elbow in his side trying to tickle him into a smile. He was slightly thinner and my hair was longer back then. We look so happy.

"It's my favorite too," Greg says, looking into my eyes, reading my mind again. "See how happy we look?" He takes a seat next to me and smiles.

"I thought you lost this picture. You said you lost—"

"I found it a while ago. I was going to save it for our first wedding anniversary."

I can't help but smile. "I'm much more prettier now," I say in a soft, playful voice.

"...No. You were *beautiful* then and you're *beautiful* now," he says, gently laying me down on the bed after we kiss. Moving quickly, as if hurrying before I can change my mind or sort out the details, he wastes no time taking off his clothes and mine. With little resistance, I let his body cover me. His lust and the thought of getting even with Leron gets me excited. I want to see the look on Leron's face when I tell him I spent the night with Greg. "I want you so bad, you don't understand," Greg breathes into my ear, sweaty cheek against my face. "You want me?"

Soon as I hear those words 'You want me,' my arms and legs grow tense and my mind drifts. What am I doing here? I've felt Greg's lips, hands, and breath on my body before. I shouldn't be tense at all. But I am. "You want me, baby. I know it." He's so focused on telling me what I want that he doesn't notice anything: the blank expression on my face, my stiff body, or the tears forming in my eyes. I don't *want* him. But I stop myself from pushing him off of me. I guess this is my way of getting even with Leron.

"Uh huh..." I mutter while thinking of Leron and the lies I know he's going to make up when I tell him I know about Ann.

19

I'm glad to see 'Welcome to Manchester Regional Airport' on the wall. Whenever I fly from Atlanta to New Hampshire, I usually get antsy after the first hour. But it's over now and I made it safely. Ain't too many people here, nobody has bumped into me with their luggage or anything. It's quiet too. I'd feel like I was in a library if it wasn't for the announcements on the loudspeakers. I head straight for the exit. I didn't have to claim any baggage 'cause all I brought is a big gym bag and a backpack. I don't like packing heavy—half the time I don't even use everything. Munching on some pretzels from the flight, I head towards the exit. Femia's parked on the curb, I can see her car from the lobby. She's always been punctual. I can't say that about too many other chicks. I walk to the car, she's messing with the radio and doesn't notice me smiling, tapping on the window. When she finally sees me, she jumps outta the car like the engine is on fire, and skips over to greet me. I see she gave up her long hair for a stylish bob cut that tapers in the back.

"RON!" she shouts, grabbing me like a Pro Bowl linebacker.

"Fefe! It's so good to see you."

Holding my hands, she steps back. "Look at you!" But I'm not trying to look at *me*, I'm trying to look at *her*! I dunno what happened! I expected her to look slightly different, but she's completely changed since the last time I saw her. She used to be skinny as a spaghetti noodle. But now her hips are shapelier, her breasts are bigger, good Lord, her body is boomin' for real. Her slender build makes her appear taller than she is—she looks more like a track star than a mathematician. I'm trying my best not to stare. I don't wanna be so obvious. But, WHOA!

"Girl, you look good! What you been eating?"

"Everything! That's why I'm so fat!"

"Fat? Please! Fat in the right places," I laugh.

She slaps my shoulder. "Boy, get in the car!"

I load my stuff and hop inside, immediately pushing the seat back for legroom.

"I see you still pushin' the Corolla."

"Yup! I'm going to drive it until the wheels fall off too!" She's been driving this car since she was seventeen. Every time I joke about it, she tells me she doesn't wanna be stuck with new car payments until she starts working.

"Girl, the way this thing is wobbling, that might be soon—all the miles you put on this sucker."

She pets the dashboard. "So! My baby is still holding up—ain't that right Betsy Mae?"

"Besty Mae? Your car looks like a Shaquesha to me!" We crack up laughing. "Oh, I brought the rough draft of my book. You can peep it when you get time."

"You sure don't sound too excited about it."

"I am, I just don't think it's hit me yet, my mind's been pretty occupied."

"What did Michelle say when you told her you were coming?" Femia asks, glancing at my facial reaction.

"She's a woman, so of course she asked a few questions about you—nothing serious, though. But if she saw how good you looked, she might've tried to keep me hostage!"

"Whatever, boy! At least she trusts you, that's good."

"Yeah, I trust her too. She wouldn't do anything behind my back."

▼

Femia's crib is small but not as small as her old dorm room. She leaves for Dallas in a few days, so it's kinda empty looking in here. If it wasn't for the neatly packed and labeled boxes everywhere, I'd think the place was abandoned.

"This is the living room, there's the kitchen, the dining room is over there, and these are the walls," she says pointing to each area, "Okay, that's that..."

We walk to her room. It looks like a big garage sale is about to start. Clothes are stacked on the bed, some on hangers, some folded; all of her pens, pencils, markers, folders, and junk like that are in a brown milk crate on the desk; sitting on a tall wooden chest is a thirteen-inch combo TV/VCR with the cord wrapped around it; and on the room door is a wall calendar with tomorrow's date circled in red marker.

"...Here's my room and there's the bathroom—okay, the tour is over!" she smiles.

I stick my hand out. "I want my money back!"

"We have a no refund policy, sorry," she says, slapping my hand.

"You gotta lot of stuff, girl." I look around the room and wonder how in the world can one person can have so much stuff, and half of it is books!

"This isn't much. Most of my things are at my parents' house."

I nod and look at a picture of a lil' boy kissing a lil' girl on the wall.

"That reminds me of you and I every time I look at it," Femia says, "Remember how you used to always chase me around the playground?"

"You mean *you* used to chase me!"

"I never chased you! You used to always ask me to be your girlfriend and I always said no."

I shake my head. "If you say so..."

"Boy!" Femia walks to the closet and pulls outta plastic container full of papers. "Here, read this." She hands me a half torn note written in black crayon. I read the poorly written words out loud.

"...You are very cute. Can we get marry? Yes or no." I start cracking up. It's a note I wrote in first grade. "I can't believe you still have this thing."

"Of course I do, it's my very first love letter."

"Yeah, I had smooth game back then," a big smile spreads across my face. "But it took three lollipops and a chocolate snack cake to get you to say yes."

Femia sticks out her lips, playfully rolls her neck and in the most ghetto voice she can imitate says, "I had to make you earn my love, honey baby!"

Later on, she takes me through my old neighborhood to show me how the place has changed. Two streets over from where I used to live was an empty lot where we played kickball and tag. Next to it was a lil' store with a laundromat. All of that is gone, replaced by new houses. We pass by our old elementary school and I didn't recognize it. It looks like a community college now: they added more buildings and the parking lot is bigger. After that, we grab some food but have to hurry and eat fast. She has to go back out to the airport to pick up some more of her friends. They said they wouldn't be able to make it to the graduation so they could surprise her when they actually did come. Femia apologizes and says she wishes she could spend more time with me tonight. I understand, though. They probably gonna go to a club or do some girly thing. I don't feel like rollin' out with a bunch of nerdy chicks anyway. She can just drop me off at Joe's crib. I'll have him take me to her parents' house in the morning.

▼

I arrive with Femia's parents at the Manchester Civic Center thirty minutes before the ceremony starts. The seats are uncomfortable, feels like my butt is made of wood. It seems like hours pass before they actually begin calling names. It's taking forever to reach the "W's." Waiting all this time just to hear one name get called is pure torture. I forgot how long and boring graduation ceremonies are. But

I can suffer through it—it's Femia's big day. I start dozing off a lil' when they finally call her name: Femia Watts. She glides across the stage, gets her degree, and struts off like an academy award-winning actress. She's straight up sassy with it too. When the ceremony ends, the first thing she asks is where do I wanna party. I tell her I'll decide after we hang with her family and friends. Today is her day, not mine. Then everyone heads to her parents' house to eat, socialize, and celebrate some more. The house still looks the same: white with a wooden fence. Inside, Femia's trophies, plaques, awards, and pictures are displayed for all to see; music is playing and everyone is having a ball. Lil' kids are chasing each other in and outta the house; grown ups are mingling in circles talking about sports, politics, and the fluorescent hat a lady wore to church last Sunday. Every time I breathe, I smell a new dish in the air. I haven't seen this much food since my family celebrated my uncle getting outta prison. Fried chicken, barbecue chicken—not tofu, baby back ribs, honey-baked ham, macaroni and cheese, black-eyed peas, collard greens, turnip greens, candied yams, potato salad, cornbread, sweet potato pie, banana pudding—lord have mercy, the table is loaded! Most of her people are big-boned, they're used to eating good. My frozen dinners and red punch ain't got nothing on this! Everything is set up buffet style. After fixing a plate, I just kinda roam around until I find an empty folding chair next to an older couple. They keep looking at me funny. I smile to acknowledge their existence, before cramming some black-eyed peas in my mouth.

"You're Frank's son, aren't you?" the man asks with cornbread crumbs sticking in the corners of his mouth. When he talks, they take off like heat-seeking missiles. I hope none of them land in my plate.

I respectfully smile. "Yes."

"Last time I saw you, you couldn't even walk without falling down." I smile again and think, *I hope this man don't talk me to death, I'm hungry!* "Goodness gracious, you look just like your Daddy." He taps his wife on the shoulder, "Sophie, doesn't he look just like Frank?"

"The spitting image."

He leans back with a hand in his lap. "Your daddy and I played basketball together. We used to call him 'Frank the tank.' When he set a pick, it was like running into a brick wall. Tell him Raymond said 'hello.' Number three. He'll know who you're talking about."

"I sure w—"

Femia walks up. "Is he giving you a hard time, Uncle Ray?" I stuff more food in my mouth while they chat. She formally introduces us and says she has more people for me to meet. Sitting my full plate on the chair, I take quick gulp of tea, and follow her. I look back at my lonely plate like a mother leaving a child at daycare. *I ain't never gonna get to eat,* I groan to myself.

The living room is small and crowded. My toes have been stepped on at least five times. Femia holds my hand, pointing out different people.

"See the guy with the blue shirt? That's my daddy's best friend."

"Cool, he has a pretty daughter."

"That's his wife!"

"Oh. Pops got it going on! I hope I have it like that when I get older." Femia pinches my arm. "Ouch! What you pinch me for?" She ignores me and keeps walking. We make our way through the living room towards the kitchen.

A short, chubby lady wearing two pounds of make-up stops us. "Fefe, come here baby, give your Aunt some love!" Femia wraps her arms around the lady far as she can—which isn't very much. "How's my graduate doing?"

"I'm doing well, just happy it's over."

"I hear you, honey." She looks at me like a box of double-glazed donuts, "And who is this handsome young man?"

"This is my good friend, Leron King. He came all the way from Atlanta to see me walk."

"Did you say King?" Her aunt asks. Femia nods. "Oh my goodness, you're Dorothy's son! You look just like your mother, just like her! She and I were on the cheerleading team in high school." She holds up her arms and shouts, "Goooo team, go!"

You used to be a cheerleader? When they formed a pyramid, I just hope you were at the bottom, I snicker to myself.

"Well, you two have fun. I need to get a piece of cake before it's all gone. You know how your cousins are. They'll sit there and eat the whole thing. Tell your mother Gloria asked about her, Leron." I wave goodbye as she wobbles off into the crowd.

Femia laughs. "You'll have to excuse her, sometimes she thinks she's still in high school."

"I see."

Femia asks if I'm getting bored. I tell her that meeting the family is cool but I really came to spend time with her.

She leans on my shoulder. "Let's go outside for a while."

The muffled sounds of Kool and the Gang's *Celebration* spills from the house on to the patio deck. We are sitting together on a wooden bench.

"Some peace and quiet," she says stretching. Her hair flickers every time a breeze kisses it.

"Yeah, it's nice. I see your father finally finished this deck."

"My mother made him finish so we could use it for the party."

"Oh, so that's why," I laugh—she doesn't. "What's wrong?"

Femia folds her arms and says she's scared of leaving her family, being by herself, and failing. I pull her closer, assuring her that there's nothing to be afraid of. Everybody needs to make their own mark in life.

"...If I would've interviewed better with BCS Financial, I could've worked right here in Manchester. You know this is the biggest thing I've ever done, Leron. I guess I'm just nervous," she says. "I have no family or friends down there, I don't know anyone."

"Are you asking me to move to Dallas with you?"

"Leron, be serious."

"I'm kidding. Don't worry, though, you know I'm here for you if you need me."

"Yeah but if something happens, what are you going to be able to do way in Atlanta?"

I smirk and say, "By plane it's only two hours and thirty-two minutes from Atlanta to Dallas. That's only seven hundred thirty-one miles."

She looks at me with a sideways stare. "How do you know that?"

"I already checked it out on the internet!" We laugh, moving closer to each other.

"Have I ever told you you're a real nut?" She looks at me, smiling, "But I'm glad I have you in my life." For a split second, we freeze gazing into each other's eyes. We lean closer. WHAM! The screen door slams, interrupting the moment. Her lil' niece runs out waving a dollar bill. She's all hair and smiles—real cute, but not now!

"Aunt Fefe, Aunt Fefe. Look' it what I got."

"Look at what I have," Femia corrects her.

The lil' girl flashes her cash. "Look at what I have."

"Oh wow! What are you going to do with all that money?"

"Buy some candy," she giggles.

Somebody comes to the door to let us know the cake is about to be cut. With an apologetic look on her face, Femia glances at me before slowly getting up. I wish we could've explored this 'thing' further. I dunno what woulda happened if her sweet, adorable niece didn't interrupt us. We always shared a playful attraction but right now, it feels much stronger, powerful. Maybe it's always been there and we ignored it.

Later on when the get-together is over, we catch a late movie with some of Femia's friends and chill at a Waffle House. Afterwards, she takes me to Joe's again. He's driving me to the airport tomorrow.

▼

The sounds of parking attendants blowing whistles, car doors slamming, babies crying, and other airport noise is making me sick. I've been outside more than an hour hoping the next pair of headlights pulling to the curbside will be Michelle's. If she wasn't gonna be able to pick me up, she shoulda called. I look like a real fool out here. I know I told her 7:30 p.m. I've called her cell, house, and office, still haven't been able to reach her. I'm giving up and taking a taxi. I don't even care about the arm, leg, and two pinky fingers it's gonna cost. I just hope everything is cool with her. Anesia pops in my head. I can't help but wonder if she's done something to Michelle. After all she's done to get back at me, I don't put nothing past her. Soon as I get home, I call one more time and leave a message. Then I call Femia and leave a message saying I made it home safe. I wonder if she's been thinking about yesterday on the patio as much as I've been.

▼

Two whole days have passed. It's Wednesday night and I still haven't heard anything from Michelle. I'm at my computer with a hand to my forehead wondering what the deal is. I'm tired of leaving messages; she never responded to the first one, no sense in leaving anymore. Twice I think about doing the unthinkable. The urge presses my conscience. Should I call Anesia? Am I crazy? I glance at the phone several times and jump when it actually rings. Private number. I'm slightly paranoid at what I'll hear on the other end but I have to answer it.

"Darn! I was looking forward to leaving a message. Guess who?" asks Anesia. My heartbeat quadruples. What has she done? What is she about to tell me?

"Just say what you have to say, girl."

"Down boy, down. I'm actually calling for Michelle."

I take a deep breath. "Where is she? What did you do?"

"Relax, Leron. You think I'd do anything to hurt that sweet little girl?" As she talks, her sarcasm curdles my skin. "Michelle is very sorry she didn't pick you up. You see, last Friday after finding out she didn't get promoted...well...she killed herself."

I squeeze the phone tight. "WHAT?"

"Just joking, you're so gullible!"

"Anesia, what's going on? Stop playing games!"

"Okay," she snickers, "She didn't kill herself but she was very disappointed. When I tried to console her, I slipped and said you and I are sleeping together."

I jump from my swivel chair. "You did WHAT? That's a lie!"

"Oops! I didn't mean to lie, it was all an accident, honest. You have my Girl Scout's honor. You should have seen her face. She ran away bawling in tears. I just felt so bad for her...really I did."

"You're sick you know that? SICK!"

"Now, now, no yelling. Let's use our quiet voices, kids."

"Wait until I get my hands around your flabby neck, I'ma—"

"You know Leron, first you scrape up my brand new car and now you're threatening to strangle me? I see your mother never taught you how to treat a lady."

"Scraped your car? I didn't touch your car, what are you talking about?"

"Whatever! Don't worry about it, James has it shining like new again. If I were you, I'd be more concerned about Michelle. She's a teensy bit mad at you..."

Things are making sense now. I knew Anesia had something to do with Michelle not showing up, but I never woulda imagined this. I ain't responsible for her actions, but I still feel guilty. I knew it. If I woulda told Michelle up front about my one-night stand, things might've turned out differently. I just didn't think it mattered since it happened before our relationship began.

I brush a hand over my head. "Why are you doing this to her? She shoulda never been dragged into this." Anesia probably has an evil smile smeared across her face. My voice deepens, "You wanna hurt *me*? Then hurt *me*!"

"...I already have. AND DON'T RAISE YOUR VOICE AT ME! You shouldn't raise your voice at a pregnant woman, you might disturb the baby."

"Pregnant? Baby?"

"That's right Uncle Leron, James and I are pregnant. Isn't that wonderful?"

"Huh?"

"I'm going to be a mother! He didn't tell you? Oh, I forgot, I told him you've been trying to get with me. He's sort of mad at you too. Oopsy! Oh my, look at the time. I'm late for bible study. Goodbye."

I wanna knock something over, break something, I wanna...shoot, I dunno what I wanna do. I just want everything to be over. I drop on the bed, sitting with my hands together in front of my lips. I'll clear things up with Spurt later. Anesia is pregnant, ain't nothing I can do about that. Michelle is the main thing on my mind. I gotta go to her house. I gotta tell her the truth. I only slept with Anesia one time—

just one time, one night, and one big mistake. I only hope she'll believe me—she should, she's a rational woman, she'll understand.

20

"I don't understand...I really don't understand. Soon as I open my heart just a little bit—I get hurt, Tonya." I lean back in the corner of the sofa, trying to make sense of everything while Tonya listens to me vent. I have her full attention now that I've turned off the television. "I can't believe he was sleeping with someone the whole time—Ann at that! That's just disgusting."

Tonya folds a *Black Hair* magazine in her lap. "Michelle, you're my girl and everything, but you really shouldn't be so upset. You've been tryin' to balance two men—runnin' around to plays and cafes with Leron, and then saving Greg for a rainy day. You can't get too mad at Leron, you never fully committed to him."

"But that doesn't make what he did right. Why did he have to sleep with my boss? My boss, Tee! See, that doesn't just affect *me*, it affects my *career* too. Everybody knew I should've gotten promoted. How do I know I didn't get it because of their little sexcapades?"

"You don't, girl. This whole thing reminds me of this movie I saw where this guy—"

Tonya is cut off by a knock at the door. Whoever it is won't be staying long because I want to get back to my pity party. No one should be coming here unannounced anyway. I walk to the door, look through the peephole, and see Leron standing on the other side.

"It's him," I whisper back to Tonya. Shaking her head, she gets her purse as Leron knocks again. "Tell him 'bout his self, girl—handle yo business! Call me and lemme know what happened."

I exhale and swing open the door.

"How are you doing, Tonya?" Leron asks. Giving him a light shove, she rolls her eyes, walking past him like he's invisible. He moves aside and looks at me with a confused stare. Suddenly his eyes light up. "Baby, I'm so glad to see you. When you didn't pick me up, I thought something happened, I've been calling you like crazy and—"

"HOW DOES ANN KNOW WHERE YOUR BIRTHMARK IS?" I don't waste any time attacking—I'm hot!

"N-Now baby wait a minute. Calm down; let me...let me explain it to you. Can I come in?"

"What is there to explain, Leron? It's pretty simple to me, you screwed her—end of story."

His voice rises. "Will you just listen for a minute? Now, can I come in?" He repeats in an agitated grumble. I want to slam the door closed but I let him in and give him a chance to speak. He says he met Ann in a club before he and I met. One night he went to her house, got drunk and they had sex. I get tired of people always blaming alcohol.

"So, I guess the alcohol made you do it, right?" I ask.

"Well, see I—"

"Don't bother explaining, that was before me, I won't sweat it, but what about after that? I see you kept making the same mistake over and over again. Were you *still* drunk? Or did the devil make you do it?"

His eyebrows rise higher on his forehead. "No. No, baby. You got it all wrong. We only slept together one time. One time! If she told you anything different, it's a lie. I ain't been with anybody else since we met. I'm not even attracted to her."

"That's supposed make me feel better?"

Leron shakes his head, sighs, and continues telling me what happened. I know he's telling the truth when he says Ann bought a surround system with his credit card. I remember her mentioning something about a sound system a while back. This is just great. I was doomed from the start. I never had a chance of getting promoted. I knew something wasn't right about Ann; I just couldn't put my finger on it.

"Why didn't you tell me all this when you found out she was my boss?" I ask.

He grabs my right hand and looks me in the eyes. "I didn't think it really mattered, baby. And I didn't wanna make you feel uneasy. If I woulda known things were gonna turn out like this I—"

I ease my hand out of his. "But if you would've told me earlier, maybe I could've asked to be reviewed by someone else—someone less involved in my personal life."

"I know. I just—I know..."

"This is why I rather deal with men bosses," I huff, walking to the living room to sit down, Leron follows. "At least there's never a doubt where they stand. Women are too conniving and deceitful. But she's going to get what's coming to her I guarantee that!"

"I'm sorry about all this. I thought I was protecting you. Everything just backfired."

"No apologies needed. If anyone needs to say they're sorry, it's me. I shouldn't have flown off the handle without knowing the whole story." This time I grab his hand, hold it tight and continue, "It's just that... I really care about you, honey, and when I thought you betrayed me...I don't know, I just lost it." Then I went and slept with Greg. How am I going to break this to Leron?

"I understand. I probably woulda did the same thing. So, is everything cool now?" he asks, caressing the side of my face.

"...Yes, everything is fine," I answer but that's a lie. "Actually, there is something else, baby."

"What is it, sweetness?" he asks innocently, kissing my hand.

Slowly opening my mouth, I force out the words. "...I...I was feeling down when I found out I didn't get promoted...and when Ann told me she'd been sleeping with you, I was hurt and confused. I mean, you have to understand; I had two bombs dropped on me within minutes..." I keep pausing when I speak. I know I'm rambling but this isn't easy.

"Yeah, I understand that, honey. But is there something else? If she did something else, let me know 'cause I'll—"

I squeeze his hand tighter. "...Well, baby...Friday night Greg and I went to dinner...and afterwards... we...we made love." I swallow hard and wait for him to explode. He releases my hand, stands up without saying a word. It's silent. Scary silent. He walks to the door, stops, and paces back. It seems like a decade passes before he speaks.

"...What did you just say?"

I hate when people ask me to repeat something I never wanted to say in the first place. But it's out in the open. I say it again. "...I slept with Greg—but only because I was feeling low and thought you were sleeping with Ann. I guess it was my way of coping."

"You mean to tell me soon as things get a lil' bumpy, you forget my feelings and just go hopping in bed with him?"

I stand up to look him eye to eye. "Leron, I can ex—"

"And then you had the nerve to yell at me about Anesia," he massages the back of his neck, "What's going through your head, woman? Seriously! I knew it. I knew I shouldn't have gotten involved with you. I guess all that stuff about me being THE GUY was just talk?"

He jerks back when I reach for his hand again. "No, I really meant it, I honestly planned on telling Greg we were through. I was going to tell him about you and I. I was. But then all these things started happening and—"

He slams a hand against the wall. "And you dropped your panties and opened your legs!"

"Leron, that's not fair!"

"Well, what do you want me to say, Michelle—that I don't care, that maybe we can work it out?"

"Well, maybe."

"C' mon, be serious," he shakes his head as if shaking the thought from his mind. "It'll never work." He sounds completely disgusted at the idea.

"Leron, please. Put yourself in my shoes. How do you think I feel?"

"I dunno. I guess you felt pretty good while he was sticking it to you."

I gather myself and speak as calmly as possible. "Okay, fine. Take cheap shots, I deserve it. It's my fault. Before we met, my life was already chaotic and I pulled you into it. I should've known better." I pat my eyes when I feel moisture forming.

Leron stares off into space. "...No, it's not all your fault. I'm an adult." His voice softens, "I can make my own decisions. I should've known better too. So what now?" he asks, leaning against the wall. He won't even look me in the face anymore. I fold my arms to keep from feeling awkward. "I guess you're gonna start wearing your ring again—y'all patched things up and all."

"I'm not sure, my head is spinning. Too much has happened too fast. I just need to wait for the smoke to clear, and then I'll figure out what to do next. What about you?"

"I dunno. I think I'll take a break from the dating game for a while; take things one day at a time, see what happens."

"Well, I'm really glad I met you—if that's worth anything—you taught me a lot about life and myself, lessons I'll never forget." He finally looks at me but doesn't say anything. I release a light sigh. "Can I still get an autographed copy of your book?"

"...Sure," he mumbles.

"...Good," I kiss his cheek. "I'll keep in contact with you from time to time to see how you're doing. Will you do the same?"

"Yeah," he says but I know he won't—I probably won't either. People always say they'll keep in touch, and maybe for the first few months they do, but then it stops. I guess it just sounds good to the ears. Leron says goodbye and walks out. Immediately, I close the door. I can't bear watching him walk away. It's too painful. Tears begin falling when I hear his car door open and close. I hurry to the shower to wash away the rest before they fall.

▼

I stare at the steamy shower floor wishing all my problems would drain away like the soapy water. But they won't and I just have to deal with them. I feel empty again, just like I did before Leron and I met. Life is certainly one big circle.

Still in my robe, I turn on the television for background noise and sit down to read a magazine. My skin feels clean and refreshed. I can't say the same for my heart. What just happened? This all seems like a dream even though I'm awake. Was tonight the last time I'll see Leron? My mind runs rampant with a hundred thoughts at once; hectic like Times Square on New Year's Eve.

I thumb through the magazine pages until an article catches my eye. *Finding a Lust for Life* the title reads. It seems appropriate, but I just can't concentrate long enough to finish it. After reading the same sentence three times, I throw the magazine on the coffee table. When it falls on the floor, I don't even bother picking it up. I don't know how long I've been slumped in the corner of the sofa, aimlessly staring at the carpet. I'm hungry but too lazy to fix a salad, tired but too confused to sleep; I sit resting my hands in my lap until the chirping of the ringing telephone breaks my meditation.

"It's me girl."

"Oh..."

"I'm happy to hear your voice too," Tonya snaps sarcastically. "You were supposed to call me back. I got tired of waiting."

"I'm sorry. It slipped my mind."

"You don't sound like you did earlier. You had me thinkin' you were gonna hang Leron by his balls. What happened?"

"It's over."

"Oh. After you ripped him apart, you kicked him to the curb. That's my girl!"

"No, it just kind of...happened. There's a time for everything in life, and the time came for us to go our separate ways."

"Would you stop talkin' in riddles and speak English? What did he say? What was his excuse? Do I have to drag everything out of you?" After I tell her what happened she says, "If all this is just a misunderstanding, why did you two break it off?" This time I don't hesitate answering.

"Because I slept with Greg while Leron was out of town."

"YOU WHAT?" Tonya's high-pitch voice goes higher. "How come you're just now telling me this?"

"Well, it's not something I'm proud of, Tee. Should I be bragging about it?"

"No but...I dunno, I'm just really surprised. You and Greg back together now?"

"No. I just had a weak moment. That's all. I need to do a little more soul searching. I don't want Greg to get the wrong idea. I'll talk to him about it."

Michael T. Owens

▼

The next day I woke up at 7:00 a.m., my usual time but I haven't bothered getting dressed for work. Instead, I've been buried under the sheets, hiding from daylight. I didn't get much rest. I stayed up half of the night trying to sort things out. I think I'll stay home again even though today is Thursday, and I've called in sick everyday this week. I don't want to see Ann's face—no telling what I'll do to that woman. Even if I do go to work, I just know I'll pass out at my desk—although I can care less about my job at this point. Besides, I haven't taken a day off in seven months.

I finally get up and spend most of the day doing little things around the house like repotting my plants, dusting, and reading home decorating magazines to keep my mind occupied. Around ten-thirty at night, when every magazine I own has been read, all my chores and errands are complete, my conscience goes wild again. A few times, I've caught myself looking at the telephone. Maybe if I look at it long enough, magically, somehow Leron will call. But even if he does call, what will he say?

And what about Greg? I've called him twice tonight because I want to resolve things once and for all but I keep getting his voice mail. He's probably home, but he never answers calls when he's working on projects. Before I know it, I'm merging onto I-285, driving to his townhouse in the Vinnings. What's scary is I don't remember getting in the car.

I make sure to actually drive the speed limit, giving myself time to think. Concentrating on the lines on the road, I rehearse what I want to say. Practicing makes me feel more comfortable even though the words will never flow like I plan. "Last Friday was a mistake; I was weak and vulnerable," that's the first thing I'll say. Then I'll tell him about Leron. After that, I'll officially end everything. I have the perfect line too. "I'm in a selfish state of mind right now, and I don't want to share myself with anyone." Okay, I have it down. I'm ready.

Pulling alongside the house, I notice his car. I'm relieved he is home and glad I didn't drive all the way here for nothing. Taking a deep breath, I walk up the gravel path leading to the front door and knock. He doesn't answer. Waiting a minute or so, I knock again. No answer. I'm not leaving here without talking to him. Looking around to see if anyone is watching me, I reach into a frog-shaped flowerpot sitting on the window ledge. He keeps a key there for emergencies— and this *is* an emergency! I open the door and go inside.

The aroma of cinnamon candles float in the air. *I didn't know he had scented candles*, I think to myself, walking through the kitchen towards the den. The lights are off but the television isn't. Some game show is on. I hear Claude Debussy's *Prelude to the Afternoon of a Faun*, leaking from the bedroom. Whenever he has a serious project, he plays classical music to relax. I've heard this piece a couple of times but never realized all the weird sounds in it. A strange feeling claws my spine while I tiptoe to the bedroom. Peeping through the cracked door confirms my instincts. Panting and grunting, Greg is perched on some bimbo, bucking out of control. Pushing the door completely open, I walk in. They don't notice me until the door bangs against the wall. He jumps off of the girl, surprised. Turning off the stereo, he immediately begins stuttering.

"M-Michelle! Baby, I-I—" His mouth is wide open and his eyebrows are raised high. He looks like a twelve year-old boy caught with a Playboy magazine by his mother. Too shocked, I don't even hear him talking.

"TONYA?" I yell. She sits up looking stupid, covering herself with the satin sheets I bought as a Valentine's gift for Greg and me. Launching forward, I swipe at her face. Greg grabs me by the arms before I can connect.

Tonya jumps back. "It's not what it looks like, Michelle!"

"Let ...me... GO, Greg!"

"Michelle, just calm down, baby."

I scratch at his arms. "My best friend? You've been sleeping with my best—MY EX-BESTFRIEND?"

"Baby, now wait a—"

"And you, Tonya! Everything we've been through...and, and you do this to me?"

"I couldn't stand seeing you treat a good man as bad as you did!" she says, fixing her hair. If I could only get to her, she wouldn't have any hair left to fix!

Greg jumps in. "What about this Leron character? Was I supposed to just sit home twiddling my fingers while you did Lord knows what with him? When were you going to tell me about that? If Tonya didn't tell me, I would've never known."

"I was waiting for the right time but I didn't go sleeping with your best friend, did I? How long has this been going on, Greg?" He looks away. "HOW LONG?"

He lets me go to scratch his head. "...Since the first week of the big contract..."

"WHAT?" I knee him in the thigh, barely missing his family jewels.

"Ah!" He buckles over, holding himself, catching his breath.

"He needed you Michelle and you weren't there for him."

"So you rushed in to take my place?" I leap at Tonya again. Greg pulls me back. "You both make me sick." I wrestle out of his sweaty arms and push away. "What's funny is I'm not all that mad at you, Greg—you're a man, I honestly believe you can't help yourself. I came here to tell you we were finished anyway. But, Tonya, I don't know what to say. We were close."

"Chelle, I didn't mean for this to happen. I'm really sorry."

"Yeah, sorry you got caught, I bet. You two can finish, I'm leaving. I don't ever want to see either of you again." I charge out the room towards the front door. Completely naked, Greg runs after me.

Tonya calls from the room. "Michelle... Michelle?"

Greg grabs my arm. "Baby, don't do this."

"LEAVE ME ALONE!" I snatch away, run out the door and get in the car. He pleads knocking on the windshield with one hand, covering himself with the other.

"Michelle? Come on baby. Michelle, it was an accident, this wasn't planned." He's standing in front of the car trying to stop me from leaving. I quickly fasten my seatbelt.

"Move, Greg!"

"Michelle, please. PLEASE!"

"You better move before I run over you!"

"Baby, turn off the car. Let's talk about it." Ignoring him, I speed down the street. Luckily for him, he moved in time. I look in the rearview mirror, watching him cover his crotch—still shouting. I'm mad but seeing him standing nude in the middle of street like a fool makes me laugh.

▼

The highway is empty for most of the ride home, which is strange since in Atlanta cars are always on the roads no matter what time it is. I roll the window down to enjoy the night air while fireflies keep me company, lighting the purple sky like neon diamonds. I should be devastated. I've been robbed of a well-deserved promotion; I'll probably never see Leron again; and I just caught my best friend sleeping with my fiancé—all in one week! I held my tears because I didn't want them seeing me cry. Now I'm alone in my car and I can't cry even if I want to. Sometimes pain can be *so* painful until it isn't painful at all. I think I'm just numb to everything.

Soon as I walk into the house, I realize I was wrong. The numbness is gone and I feel moistness in my eyes. Ignoring it, I go straight to the kitchen to get the remains of a pint of butter pecan ice cream and a bag of barbecue potato chips. Turning the television to the *Lifetime Channel*, I nestle back into my usual spot on the sofa. I've sat in this spot many times; the cushions have molded to fit the shape of my body.

I watch two *Lifetime Original Movies* and one episode of *The Golden Girls,* all of which I've seen before. None of the other channels have anything worth watching. Eleven o'clock turns into midnight, midnight quickly becomes one in the morning. Unable to fall asleep, I begin writing a poem, thinking maybe I'll get drowsy. But what begins as another poem soon becomes a "things to do" list.

1. *Write a letter of resignation*

2. *Find out the requirements for Florida teacher certification*

3. *Research real estate agents*

4. *Get estimates from moving companies*

5. *Donate anything Greg left behind to charity*

I'm writing down things I need to do to better my life—starting with quitting my job. Tomorrow I plan on calling in sick again; and Monday I'll hand in my two weeks notice. I realize life is too short to spend it unhappily slaving away in corporate America. If I have to work, I need to do something meaningful and worthwhile. That's why I'm selling my house and moving back to Florida to teach. The monetary reward isn't great, but the emotional gratification is worth more than any paycheck.

Looking at the empty ice cream container and crumpled potato chip bag, I scribble down numbers six, seven, eight, and nine.

6. *Start eating healthier*

7. *Start back working out*

8. *Start taking multi-vitamins*

9. *Go shoppi*

Before I can finish number nine—out of nowhere—they start pouring. Tears. Stinging tears. Despite my stubbornness to cry, they finally force themselves free. Pictures of Leron, Greg, Tonya, Ann, back to Leron, and then Ann again, flash in my mind. Looking at my list, I sniffle and write:

10. GET ANN!

What am I thinking? I ball up the tear-stained list, holding it tight as if trying to squeeze out the ink. "UNGH!" I grunt, throwing it across the room. I thought making a list would help clear my head— but it doesn't. I still feel lost. I still feel confused. And I'm still pissed.

21

I'm on the way to the park. It's Thursday evening and heavy-looking clouds are circling in the sky. I don't care. I just hope it doesn't rain yet. I wanna shoot around by myself to get my mind off of things 'cause I don't wanna think about Michelle right now. I did that last night. Right now, I rather work on my jump shot. I don't wanna think about Anesia either. Practicing my left-handed lay-up is more important.

After swerving into a parking spot, I hop outta the car so fast I almost slam my finger in the door. I walk faster after hearing yelling, shouting, and cursing coming from the court. Since the weather is bad, I figured no one would be out, but now I might actually get to play a full court game. I stop dead in my tracks when I hear somebody shout, "Spurt, pass the rock!" I squeeze my basketball tight while I think for a minute. *Spurt's here? Outta all the days to hoop he picks today?* I'm not ready to face him yet 'cause I know he won't listen to me. I don't even know what to say or how. Anesia's probably been telling him all kinda crazy stuff. Lies. I came out here to relax, not to get into it with Spurt. Luckily, I haven't made it up to the court yet. I can turn around and leave without him ever knowing I was here. I'll just play some other t—.

"HEEEY, LERON!" one of the regulars yells from courtside. "Wanna play next game?" I know everybody heard him—including Spurt. Man! He gotta big mouth. I can't leave now. I finish the long walk up to the court. Lots of guys are here playing but the only one I see is Spurt. He's glaring at me like he wanna dunk my head instead of the ball. And I'm looking and feeling guilty even though I didn't do anything wrong.

He shakes his head and walks off the court in the middle of a fast break. "I'm out y'all..."

"What? All we need is two more points. You can't stay for two points?" One of his teammates pleads.

"I got something to do, dawg." Thunder rumbles in the sky as he walks towards me. His sweaty face, bulging nostrils, and squinted eyes look threatening. I take a deep breath and brace myself for whatever is about to happen.

"What's up man? Where you been hiding?" I ask lightheartedly, trying to cool him off before he gets closer. Ignoring my words, he shoves me outta the way and gets his keys off the picnic table. "Spurt?"

"Don't talk to me." He walks off towards the parking lot.

"Spurt, c'mon, man..."

"If you smart, you'll leave me alone, dawg."

I stand there watching him walk to his car. A loud clap of thunder rocks the sky as he speeds off. I look back at the rest of the guys. "Are we gonna play, or stand here and wait for it to rain?"

▼

I dunno how many basketball games I played after Spurt left. But I know any guilt, frustration, or disappointments I had about all that's happened, temporarily stopped. I balled until the night-lights came on, until my legs wobbled—until the night-lights went off. The world paused until I drove outta the park gates—back to reality.

It's a lil' after 9:00 now. If I didn't have to take X and Lisa to the airport, I'd still be ballin.' Their flight leaves at 11:25 p.m. and I have no time to waste. I fix a sandwich, shower, and rush back out the door.

Man! X is leaving, I think to myself, *He's really leaving.* All my homies are leaving. The friends I've been tight with for years are moving away. My mind has been cloudy lately, things are taking longer to sink in than usual. Suddenly, two miles from X's crib everything hit me. I can't imagine how Atlanta will be without my dawgs. Slowly lifting my foot off the gas pedal, I drive the last three miles slow as possible, letting old memories bubble in my head; like when Ra's mother was put on bed rest for a week. Me and the guys all helped around the house; taking out the trash, cleaning, cooking— well, we tried. She always cooked for us, so we wanted to return the favor. We looked like some real rejects. X wore a small pink apron with the words 'Super Mom,' on the front; Spurt, Dave, and Ra had on these stupid looking hairnets; and I wore my special pimp-cooking hat. I shoulda took pictures. We were something serious!

Maybe we took it a lil' too serious.

Spurt leaned against the wall with a mixing bowl and spoon. "Dave, you ain't done choppin' 'dem carrots yet?"

Dave stood on the left side of the sink. "Almost, chill out."

"It don't take thirty minutes to cut three carrots, man. Hurry up!"

"Spurt where did you put the flour?" I asked.

"It' hasn't been thirty minutes, what are you talking about?"

"Over there."

"Where?"

"Hey, where's that thing?" X asked staring, into a steaming frying pan.

Ra looked over Dave's shoulder. "Hey you washed them first, right?"

"That thing you cook with. The flat thing." X snapped his fingers, trying to remember the name.

Confused, Dave paused for a minute. "You're supposed to wash them too?"

"That thing. You know what I'm talking about."

Ra handed X a spatula. "You mean a spatula?"

"Yeah, dummy. You suppose to wash all raw vegetables," Spurt said.

"Yeah, a spatula, thanks."

"Holding the bag of flour in my hands, I examined the label. "Ra, this is brown flour—you were supposed to get white flour. He hunched his shoulders as if to say 'so what.'

"What's the difference?" Dave asked.

"The color!" X laughed to himself.

I walked over to Dave. "Look. I'm brown, you're white, see the difference?"

"I don't think the color matters that much," he said.

"I knew white boy would say something like that," Spurt interrupted.

"Well, we don't have time to go back to the store anyway. We'll make do."

We sounded like a group of frustrated cooking school flunkies. We'd only been in the kitchen twenty minutes, but ready to strangle each other within the first ten. The meal was fabulous—well, actually, it sucked, but at the time, we thought it was a masterpiece. Mrs. Naseem said she liked it—she knew our intentions were good and didn't wanna hurt our manly egos. Looking back, that whole day was hilarious.

I'ma miss my homies. We had some wild times. I remember one night Ra was dancing with these two overweight chicks. Everybody on the dance floor moved outta the way—if you saw him dance you'd understand why. The crowd formed a circle yelling, hollering, and cheering them on. He didn't care about a thing! One girl danced in front of him and one in back—she wiggled and jiggled like an ice cube fell down her dress. Sandwiched in the middle, wildly waving his arms, Ra yelled, "Shake what yo mama gave ya," again and again. Them girls probably lost twenty pounds that night! It was too funny; and he was sober the whole time! Hands down, Ra'ed easily has more nerve than all of us. I woulda never got out there like he did. Those crazy nights are over for now. One day the five horsemen will ride again. Maybe.

Michael T. Owens

▼

My headlights shine through the window as I pull into X's driveway. Him and Lisa come outta the house before I can turn off the car. Lisa hurries to the car while X moves with the speed of a grandfather tortoise. The luggage he's toting isn't the only thing weighing him down. He's built a good life in Atlanta, only to uproot and rebuild elsewhere. I know that's probably making those bags feel heavier. He places the few things they packed in my ride. His job hired movers to move everything else to Indiana. I wonder why his company can afford to move everything across the country, but can't arrange a flight at a decent hour.

The ride is quiet for the most part. Lisa nags X about a couple of things then falls asleep. X stares outta the window and I stare at the road. The low murmur of some ridiculous talk radio show helps tame the silence. Some tipsy lady calls in talking about she was abducted by aliens. A guy after her calls in saying he can leave his body whenever he feels like it.

"These people stupid," I groan.

X grunts and continues looking outta the window. I don't expect a real response. But I just felt compelled to say something—anything. I don't bother trying to spark another conversation. I let the radio do all the talking. Eight callers and ninety-nine million commercials later, we arrive at the airport entrance.

I help X gather the bags outta the trunk. "Xavier Deshayon John Spivey III, this is it my man."

"Yeah, bro, this is it. You coming to the wedding, right?" I give him a 'what do you think' look. He pats my shoulder and grins. "Take care of yourself."

"You too, man. Take care, Lisa."

"Okay, Leron, you too. Thanks for the ride."

I can tell X hates long goodbyes as much as I do. You can only say goodbye so many ways. I give him and Lisa quick hugs and that's that. We can read between the lines. We'll miss each other. We just didn't say it in those exact words. After watching them disappear into the lobby, I drive off. I ain't listening to that crazy radio station again—it might put me to sleep. I turn the radio to V103 and hit the gas pedal.

The clouds finally let go of the rain. A light shower falls a few minutes after I leave the airport. Instead of slowing down, I keep speeding on I-75 North vibin' to my music. I check the side mirror and notice a white Ford Explorer riding a car-length behind me. I change to the center lane. He changes to the center lane. I change back to the right lane. He does the same. When I exit off on Tenth Street, he exits too.

What is this fool doing? Just before reaching the traffic light, he swerves in front of me. With no time to react, I slam into his rear, making a big horizontal dent in his truck. Smoke rises from my bent hood and one of the headlights is busted. I turn off the engine, put on the hazard lights, and I jump outta my ride to see if the dude is okay.

"Hey man, you cool? I tried to stop but you cut me—"

Another car swerves beside us. Two husky dudes jump out and rush me. I dodge one, but the other hit me with a fist to the temple.

When I stagger back, they catch me and toss me in their ride. Next thing I know, I'm in the shadows behind some rundown building getting beat down. Bloody and bruised, two dudes take turns pounding my face and stomach, while the other two hold my arms, leaving me defenseless. My legs buckle and weaken. When I stumble, they hold me back up, beating me some more. Every breath hurts and coughing hurts worse; my chest throbs with excruciating pain.

"AHHH, GOD!" I wheeze.

A muscular dude with thick dreadlocks points at me and says, "Dat's for disrepctin' muh sister!" He jabs my ribs before I can ask what he's talking about. "...And dat's for messin' with huh car, PUNK!" The other guys laugh when I beg him to stop. My body is limp but the dudes won't let me fall.

"Hold'em up. HOLD'EM UP!"

"Uhhh...please...stop..."

One of the guys yanks my arm. "SHUT UP!"

"Yo, let'em go," says the dude with the dreads, wiping rain from his face. "HA! Look at'em nah, on the ground beggin' like uh lil' faggot."

I lay in a puddle of dirty rainwater, holding my side while piss, cigarette, and sour beer odors run up my bloody nose, forcing me to cough again. I grab my chest to ease the pain. It's pouring harder, the raindrops feel like nails hammering me to the pavement. I have no vision in my left eye but through my swollen right eye I see... Spurt's car pulls up? Huh? He gets out holding a black umbrella, walks to the passenger side. Anesia gets out smiling. He walks over to me with her holding his arm and says, "So you hollerin' at my girl behind my back, huh? Payback hurt don't it?" He laughs, kisses Anesia, and they walk away.

"...Spurt...w-w-why man...uhhh...?" I pass out.

▼

Glaring lights blind me when I open my eyes. A siren-like sound rings in my head; a piercing pain shoots down my side. I hear several voices but can't figure out what they're saying. I try to get up but I'm strapped to a bed.

"Sir, try not to move," says an unfamiliar male voice. I scan my surroundings. Two paramedics and a cop huddle over me. I think I'm in an ambulance.

"...What's going on? What happened?" I ask.

"Relax, sir. Just relax." The officer pulls out a pen and pad, "A jogger found you unconscious on the side of Piedmont Avenue and called us immediately. Do you remember anything?"

I concentrate; my brain feels like grape gelatin. The first thing to pop in my head is Spurt and Anesia standing over me. Slowly everything else comes to memory. "Uh...it was about eleven something, I was coming back from Hartsfield...my side is killing me!"

"We know," says a paramedic, "We're almost there. Don't move."

The officer scribbles some more. "What happened then, sir?"

I motion the paramedic closer. "Gimme another of hit of that oxygen!" After filling my lungs, I finish the story. The police officer writes as fast as I can tell it.

"Okay, sir, that's all for now. Get some rest."

▼

I don't remember coming to Grady Memorial Hospital, but the nurse says I've been here since last night. The diagnosis? I gotta a tailbone contusion, three broken ribs, fractured collarbone, sprained wrist, a black eye, and an injured ego. Them big dudes whipped me good. It ain't as bad as it sounds, but the pain is ridiculous. I'm just glad the nurse is keeping me drugged up. She says my folks will be in town later tonight. I feel bad, this is the first vacation they've taken in a couple of years, and it's cut short courtesy of me.

None of the people I care about are around. X is in Indiana by now; Dave is in Africa somewhere—and just like I figured, Ra'ed ended up going too; Femia just started her new job in Dallas; and Spurt—after what he did, doesn't even exist in my eyes. How can he stand by and watch me get jumped? And all for some chick—an ugly one at that. Bored and alone, I leave the television on while I sleep to pass time. In the middle of napping, I faintly hear a woman's voice reading:

"...Last, but certainly not least, I want to thank a very special person in my life... "

Although I'm drugged and half conscious, I still recognize those words from the acknowledgement page of my rough draft. I'm straining to open my eyes but I can't. All I see is darkness. Placing a soft warm hand on my arm, she continues reading:

"...For putting up with my insanity and encouraging me to finish.

Femia, I hope you smile when you read this." She pauses to reflect on the words. "...I'm smiling, Ron, I'm smiling..." I try to open my eyes again; finally, they crack enough to see a blurry figure standing at the bedside.

"Fe...fe, is that y—?" What's she doing here? I thought she was supposed to be in Dallas.

"Shhh, don't speak. Yes, it's me. Soon as your mother called me, I caught the first flight available. I told my new boss what happened, she let me postpone my start date."

I attempt sitting up to see her better. "But—"

"Shhh," she says again. "Be still, now. The nurse says you're pretty banged up—you don't need to be trying to move. Don't worry, you'll be out soon, but it's going to take some time for you to fully heal." She pulls the sheets over my chest and sits down next to the bed. Staring at me, then the bare wall, she sighs. "I don't get it, what would make someone do this? They didn't take your wallet, your watch, *or* your jewelry. It's like they just did it for fun..."

All I can do is listen as the compassion in her voice massages my sore body.

Spurt and Anesia appear in my head, then my mind shifts to Michelle and the dream I had where the woman went back to the guy even after I fought hard for her. Michelle did the same thing. Despite our feelings for each other, she went back to Greg anyway.

Femia enters my thoughts too. Fantastic Femia. Being myself is good enough for her, I don't have to use pick-up lines or flattering comments to impress her. She cares about me. I'm helpless, in pain, at the lowest point of my life, and she's by my side holding my hand.

22

Tonight I've told myself a hundred times: *Michelle, get off of this sofa and get in the bed*! But the low mumble of television inside and the soothing sound of rain pouring outside make me want to keep laying here. Maybe the next time I fall asleep I'll *stay* asleep instead of nodding in and out like I've been doing for the last hour.

"OH MY GOD!" I gasp out loud after hearing the clang of shattering glass immediately followed by the security system sirens. Jumping from the sofa, I run to see what's going on. "Oh...my...god..." In the center of my window is a gaping two-foot hole. My mind flip-flops: *Okay, okay. Should I call the police? Yes. Call the police then turn off the alarm. No, wait Michelle. Turn off the alarm then call the police. No. I don't know!* The blaring squeal of the sirens is deafening. I can hardly think straight. *The code, the code, what is the stupid code?* After fumbling over the keypad and finally shutting off the alarm, I hear squealing tires outside. I run back to the window and catch a glimpse of a BMW speeding around the corner—Ann's red BMW. In a daze of disbelief, I stare out of the broken window, fighting the urge to get in my car and drive after her.

The phone rings.

I almost trip and fall over a red brick on the floor when I go to answer. It's the security system company. I tell them I'm fine and uninjured. They say an officer should be here any minute. I hang up and quickly walk back to the living room to inspect that brick. Taped to it is a sheet of notebook paper with the word WHORE written in black marker. Whore. W...H...O...R...E! Each letter slaps me in the face. I ball my fist tight. "That's it, Ann! Where are my keys?"

The phone rings.

"OOOUCH!" I accidentally cut my hand on a piece of glass. "Why am I so clumsy?" I whine.

The phone rings again. I look around for something to wipe the blood trickling down my wrist.

The phone rings again.

"I'm coming," I say, wiping my hand on my shirt. "I'm COMING! Hello?" I hear deep breathing on the phone then a loud outburst of laughter. It's Ann.

Now someone is knocking at the door.

"I'LL BE THERE IN A SECOND!" I yell. "Ann listen to me, I don't know what you're thinking but—" She hangs up.

Again, there's a harder, more urgent knock at the door. I open it without checking to see who it is first.

"Ms. Barkley?" asks a police officer wearing a gray raincoat.

"Yes..."

He looks at my sleepless eyes, bloody shirt, and sweaty forehead. "What happened, ma'am?"

"Well, see—" I hesitate before telling him about Ann, the brick, or the note. I don't think I want the police involved in this. Ann has gone out of her way to ruin my life. If the police catch her, she will only get a slap on the wrist, pay a fine, and that's it—that's too easy. I can personally do more harm to her than a silly fine. I put my hand on my hip and tell the officer a kid threw a rock through my window and ran. The officer nods, then points at the blood on my shirt. "...I cut myself cleaning up the mess. I'm fine."

"Sure?"

"Yes."

"I wish parents would keep their kids in line. I get calls like this everyday."

"Kids will be kids..." I smile. "Well, thanks for stopping by, I need to get back to cleaning up."

The officer tips his hat and walks to his car.

I close the door and immediately find the list I threw across the room earlier. The cut in my hand stings as I unfold the piece of paper. With a bloody finger, I trace over number ten and smirk to myself, *Ann, Ann, Ann, you've done it now.* Tomorrow when she leaves to get her lunchtime smoothie, I'll follow her and give her what she deserves.

23

"It's burning up, why is it so hot in here?" Femia asks. "And look at these dusty curtains, they probably have all kinds of germs and they call this a hospital—are you hungry? Yuck, never mind, this Salisbury steak looks like it might grow legs any minute," she rambles as if to distract her mind. "...and why are they giving you cold food anyway...Ron, everything's going to be all right," she whispers, wiping away tears before they fall. It sounds like she's convincing herself more than me.

After watching television for a while, she gets restless. "My goodness, this stupid TV only gets one channel?" she huffs while we listen to the 12:00 p.m. news:

"...In today's local news, a fatal car accident kills one and injures two Atlanta residents. Daniel Peters is reporting live from the scene...Dan?"

"Thanks Linda. It's a rainy Friday afternoon and I'm live at the scene of a car accident that occurred earlier today at the intersection of Hammond Drive and Ashford-Dunwoody Road. Michelle Barkley of Dunwoody apparently lost control of her Toyota Avalon, striking the passenger side of Ms. Anesia Mason's BMW, killing her instantly..."

Stunned, I continue listening, holding Femia's hand tighter.

"...Ms. Barkley, who sustained neck injuries and a broken leg, was airlifted to the North Fulton Medical Center and is currently in stable condition; no charges have been filed as of yet."

"Daniel, were any passengers in the vehicles?"

"Ms. Mason did have one passenger; James Gibson of Decatur. He was treated for minor injuries at Northside Hospital and is expected to be released later today."

"Looking at the condition of those cars, it's amazing how *anyone* survived, Daniel."

"You're right, Linda, it's amazing indeed. Clean up crews expect to have everything cleared by this evening. I'm Daniel Peters, reporting live for channel seven news at twelve..."

After hearing the news, I feel...I dunno—weird—not happy or sad, just...weird. Femia strokes my hair as we share silence. Psychically, mentally, and emotionally, her touch gives me peace. I wanna hold her like the woman I rescued in my other dream. The one I adored. The one I wanted to protect. The one I fell in love with. I never told Femia my feelings 'cause I wasn't sure, but now I am—I love her. Pain, aches, and broken bones don't matter—I have to tell her.

I lean to the side of the bed and mumble, "I...l-l-love...y-you..."

"Awww, Leron!" This time her tears fall freely. But these tears are different, magical—trickling from her glowing face, they vanish, never hitting the ground. "I love you too."

▼

I wake up the next morning to the most beautiful sound I've heard in a long time—Femia sitting beside the bed snoring, still holding my hand. She wakes up shortly after I do and kisses me. "I hope you slept well because I sure didn't, my neck is killing me. How do you feel—?"

A knock at the door interrupts. I hope it's the nurse bringing breakfast. I strain my ears to listen to the conversation.

"Hello, I'm James. Well, Spurt to Leron, I'm his best friend." My skin tightens after hearing Spurt at the door calling me his best friend. He doesn't know the meaning of a best friend. A best friend is with you until the end. A best friend won't let you get beat down by a bunch of thugs. He ain't my best friend.

"Ohhh, Spurt! Come in, he'll be excited to see you. I heard about the accident on the news yesterday. I'm so glad you're okay. I'm Femia, a childhood friend of Ron's. It's nice to finally meet you." If Femia knew the whole story about what happened, she'd kick him outta here without thinking twice. If I had the strength, I'd do it myself. "Leron, Spurt's here!" she sounds happy. She thinks I actually wanna see him. Wrong. I quickly close my eyes and pretend I'm sleeping so he'll get outta here. "Ron? Ron? He's asleep, Spurt. I was just talking with him a minute ago, I guess his medicine is kicking in."

From the corner of my eye, I see Spurt walking towards me. He carefully takes a seat beside the bed, making sure he doesn't bump the cast on his arm. He has a look on his face that I've never seen. His face is long and fragile, he keeps blinking his eyes almost as if he's trying hard not cry. He looks me over, shakes his head slowly and turns to Femia.

"Um...Femia?" There's a long pause before he continues. "...Uh, I-I can't stay long. But when he wakes up can you give him a message for me?"

"Sure."

"...All you gotta tell'em is...I found her diary. It was all in there..." He turns to look at me again, blinking faster than before. "...It was all in there, dawg. I know the truth now and I'm sorry. I'm sorry, man." He puts a hand over his face to hide the tears. Femia hands him a tissue. "I shoulda stopped them. I shoulda stopped them from doing this to you, dawg. I just—"

"Wait a minute! What are you talking about?" Femia stands straight up as if someone threw freezing water in her face. "You could've stopped this from happening? You could've stopped this and you didn't do anything?" Spurt looks at her then hangs his head without answering. "HOW COULD YOU!" With the tissue box in her hand, Femia beats his arms, chest, shoulders, and everything else she can reach. Tissues fly all over the place. "HOW COULD YOU?" Spurt stands to his feet, wiping his eyes, letting Femia hit him until she gets tired. "Get out of here, Spurt!" She pats tears from her eyes. "Go!"

"...I'm sorry. I—"

"LEAVE!"

I can't fake being sleep anymore. "No..."

Femia and Spurt freeze.

"You awake! I gotta tell you something, dawg."

"He doesn't want to hear anything you have to say so just g—"

"I...heard you..." I mumble.

Femia rolls her eyes and leaves the room when Spurt sits back down. "I know I've done some stupid things, but this...I'm embarrassed," his voice trembles, "If you don't wanna speak to me no more I'll understand..." I start feeling light all over and it's definitely not the morphine. The heaviness I've been carrying around has disappeared. I never heard his voice sound like this, humble and soft. I know it took a lot for him to even show up here after all that's happened. "...Will you forgive me?" he asks. I stare at him without saying a word. I'm relieved he knows Anesia was lying but I dunno if I can forgive him. He believed some chick's story without ever asking me about it. That's hard to swallow. He's waiting for my answer but I don't have one. "...Okay," he stands, clears his throat, and walks towards the door. "I don't blame you."

Before I can stop it, my mouth opens by itself. "...Spurt..."

He turns around and walks to the bed. "Yeah?"

I take a deep breath and look at my homie. "...We're cool...but I want my hundred dollars back..."

We both smile.

ABOUT THE AUTHOR

Michael T. Owens double-majored in Sociology and Communications for Business at Florida State University. After graduation, he moved to Atlanta to take a job in the Marketing Communications field. A year later, he began writing *Pick-Up Lines*. He now resides in central Florida and is busy working on various projects. Visit his website: www.michaeltowens.com or email him at: michaeltowens@yahoo.com.